Margaret Mendel

PUSHING TIME PRESS

ISBN: 978-0-578-39842-6
ebook ISBN: 978-0-578-39843-3

First printing: 2017 Muse It Up Publishing

For information, please contact the author:
margaret_mendel123@yahoo.com

To Steven,
my inspiration,
my muse.

Chapter One

SHARON SAT IN A SMALL patch of sunshine outside Willie's weigh station, resting her back against a scrubby pine tree, face raised to the warm light. The heat from the afternoon sun dulled her mind like a drug. The end of summer was unseasonably warm this year on the Kenai Peninsula. The Alaskan fireweed had already finished an early bloom, which meant the first snowfall could come any time now. Sharon wondered where she'd go when it turned cold.

A pickup truck loaded with a fresh catch of salmon rambled up the road and backed into the weigh station. Open net fishing season, and a short run of excess salmon during spawning season, put into play a frenzy of underemployed men and women scrambling for the mother lode of sockeye and reds heading up stream and into the interior. Willie owned a stretch of land on a bluff overlooking Cook Inlet, and in the summer, he turned an old shed on his property into a weighing station and became a middleman for the fish canneries.

"Sharon!" Willie called.

He didn't need to shout. She knew her job. But he was the head honcho and she figured he thought all seasonal workers were lazy and stupid. And by the way he hollered, she'd begun to think he probably thought they were all hard of hearing, too.

"Herb!" Willie called for his son, the only other person, beside himself, that the old man allowed to drive the forklift. "Herb!"

The last couple of days, the old man appeared to think his offspring might have gone hard of hearing too.

She stood, headed for the weigh station, and waited for the son to show up.

The driver of the pickup turned off the engine. Cigarette smoke billowed out of the open door of the truck as the tail end of an old country song blasted out from the radio. The driver climbed down from behind the steering wheel and stretched his back.

"I don't know, Willie. I'm getting too old for this shit." He reached into the cab of the truck and turned off the radio.

"Real men don't stop fishing, you know that, Jake," Willie said.

"Suppose so," Jake said. "It just seems to be getting harder every year."

Sharon stepped into the weigh station.

Jake nodded to her. "Morning."

She nodded back, leaned against a far wall, and waited.

Jake looked around the weigh station, nervously fidgeting with his sweat-stained baseball cap. "Is this going to take all day? These fish won't stay fresh forever."

"Herb!" Hands on his hips, Willie glanced at Sharon with an exasperated look.

She didn't respond, had no intention of getting involved with any trouble brewing between father and son. But it was clear from the first day she'd met Herb that he had taken an instant dislike for her. He was a mean-spirited young man, and all she wanted to do now was put in her time until the end of the open net season and then get the hell out of there.

When Herb finally sauntered into the weigh station, he gave no apologies or excuses and climbed into the forklift. He jostled the vehicle back and forth a couple of times until he positioned a large wooden crate just below the tailgate of Jake's pickup. Sharon climbed onto the bed of the truck and slogged across the slippery mound of fish.

Willie unlatched the tailgate and called up to Sharon, "All right. Let 'em go." He backed away from the truck.

Sharon's official job title was Fish Kicker. She was hired to kick, push, and shove the fish off the truck beds and into the waiting crates.

She'd gotten pretty good at it. Her stout, muscular legs gave her an advantage as she walked atop a pile of salmon. Being on the short side with a lower center of gravity had its advantages too. A taller person would have had difficulty balancing as she scrambled over the slippery mess, but Sharon quickly got the cargo moving. Her arms were as strong as any man's after all the years she'd spent chopping wood and hunting with her father and brothers. She'd gotten even stronger when she'd worked as a cook and river guide rowing the rafts up and down the Kenai River, maneuvering the white water rapids.

She scrambled across the load of salmon and quickly removed most of the fish from the bed of the truck into the cargo boxes. When there was no longer the natural slime of other dead fish to easily move the creatures, Sharon resorted to kicking individual fish into the crate. By this point, the fish were no worse off for the treatment. Once they got as far as the Cook Inlet, most salmon had already been roughed up by their ocean voyage. The salmon were a windfall for the Beluga, seals, and other large predatory feeders in the waters along the Alaskan coast. It wasn't unusual to see a salmon with a missing tail, a fin snipped off, or even a bite taken out of the belly.

Sharon jumped out of the empty bed of the pickup just as the local sheriff's car pulled into the driveway. The sheriff had been around plenty this season, and no matter what the weather, he wore a pair of ridiculous sunglasses, the kind with rainbow mirror lenses. Sharon never trusted people who lived with their eyes hidden.

"How you doing, Willie?" the sheriff asked.

"Can't complain. What's going on, Allen? You come by to get some fish?"

"Just checking with places along the inlet to see if anyone saw something out of the ordinary in the last couple of days." Sheriff Allen peered into the crate of salmon sitting at the entrance to the weigh station. "Fishy smelling place, ain't it?" The sheriff then looked at Sharon. "You this year's fish kicker?"

"Yep." It sounded more like she'd taken a bite out of the air than actually commented. He'd seen her plenty this summer, but he'd never paid her any attention until today.

"Where you from?" he asked.

Sharon heard the suspicion in his voice. She shrugged her

shoulders. "Up north."

"How far?"

"The North Pole."

"What's going on, Allen?" Willie asked.

Sheriff Allen cleared his throat and removed his sunglasses. Large, puffy circles hung beneath his charcoal black eyes. "One of the fish nets pulled up more than fish early this morning. Someone caught a dead guy. The crabs and sea lice got to him before he was snagged by a fishnet, but it was the bullet hole that made us take notice." Sheriff Allen paused for a moment, probably waiting for a response. Then he continued, "You hear about any trouble in the area?"

"Sorry. Can't help you out, Allen. Only one other load besides this one came in today. Haven't heard anything about a dead guy."

"How about you, fish kicker," the sheriff asked, "you see anything suspicious?"

"If I did, you'd be the first one I'd tell," Sharon said. She grabbed up a garden hose, turned on the spigot, and washed the slime from her boots.

"Looks like you got a feisty fish kicker on your hands, Willie. Well, if you hear anything, let me know." Sheriff Allen turned and headed out the door of the weigh station, but then he stopped and looked into the open window of the pickup truck. "You're mighty quiet, Jake."

"I've been up all night. Don't feel much like talking."

"Did you hear anything about this trouble?"

"Nope. Haven't heard a thing."

Sheriff Allen glanced at the cell phone sitting on the dashboard. "I thought you boys out on the water kept the cellular antennas humming day and night with gossip and bad jokes."

"Battery's dead. Like I told you, Allen, I don't know anything."

Sheriff Allen slipped on his sunglasses. "Well, you get home safe, Jake." He walked to his patrol car.

When the sheriff was out of hearing range, Willie said, "Don't be such a smart ass, Sharon. It's bad for business."

"You want me to be polite to the local dick, pay me more. Six bucks a truck doesn't give you anything but my stubby old legs to do some kicking, and that's all."

Willie grunted and headed for the back of the shed where he sat down at a desk consisting of two saw horses and a rough sheet of plywood. He punched at the keys of an ancient adding machine, tallying the last haul. He scribbled a few figures on a slip of paper and handed it to Jake.

"You look like shit, Jake," Willie said. "Go home. Get some rest."

Jake took the paper, climbed into his pickup, turned on the radio and headed out to the main road.

"Herb! Where's that lazy son of mine? Herb! Get your ass in here."

Several minutes later, Herb stepped into the weigh station.

"Where the hell did you run off to?" Willie snapped. "Take that crate off the scale."

"All right, all right, don't have a coronary." Herb jumped into the forklift. He removed the crate of salmon from the scale and then scooted the vehicle across the floor to a corner of the shed. "What'd the sheriff want?" Herb asked as he jumped out of the forklift.

"Looking for someone, I suspect," Willie replied, seemingly more occupied with his figures than with the sheriff's business.

"Who?" Herb asked.

"Sheriff Allen doesn't say much of anything, but it looks like he's on the trail of a murderer."

Herb turned and was almost out of the weigh station when Willie said, "Hose down the driveway out front."

"I'm busy," Herb replied. "Have the fish kicker do it. She's not doing anything."

Willie glared at his son then nodded to Sharon. The old man turned his back and continued with his bookkeeping.

Sharon picked up the garden hose and watched Herb cross the driveway to his motorcycle. It had been obvious from the start that Herb would be miserable to deal with. He treated her like dirt, and if she didn't know he wasn't worth much more than what his father gave him, you'd have thought by his actions he'd been born into royalty.

As long as the daylight held, which this late in the summer was another nine hours, Sharon sat near the weigh station, waiting for trucks to arrive loaded down with fish. When the last truck drove away, Willie locked the bay doors for the night.

"We'll start about seven tomorrow morning," Willie told Sharon and gave the padlock a yank.

Sharon nodded to the old man and then trudged out to the highway. She'd kicked a lot of fish today. Her legs were dead tired, and Willie knew she walked to and from wherever it was that she lived. No matter how late they worked, he never asked her how far she had to go or offered her a ride. But she wouldn't have told him where she lived if he asked, and she certainly wouldn't have taken a ride.

At the end of the driveway, Sharon turned left the way she always did and walked in the shallow ditch that ran alongside the highway. She kept going until she came to a narrow opening in the underbrush that led into the forest. Earlier that summer, she'd stumbled across an abandoned hunter's shelter on the bluff about a mile from the weigh station, and that's where she went every night. Nothing she ate needed refrigerating, but she'd rigged a cooler with a rope and pulley system to keep the wild animals from getting into her provisions.

She'd made a home out of a pile of boards and a couple sheets of plywood leaned up against a cluster of tree trunks with a rusty piece of corrugated metal thrown on top for a roof. The structure sat near the edge of the bluff, a strip of pebbly beach and the Cook Inlet just below. The wind could get pretty fierce up there some nights. When a squall blew across the water, the shelter usually needed a bit of anchoring the next day, though the place had kept her comfortable all summer.

Winter would be a different story. She didn't think she was tough enough to live on the bluff through the cold weather, and she had no idea where she'd end up once it started to snow. As long as she stayed away from the booze, she'd be all right. Maybe she'd head back to her mother's and see if she could get her daughter out of foster care. Or maybe she'd head the other way, go farther up north. She had no idea where she'd end up.

The visit from the sheriff today had upset her. She'd never tell him, but she'd seen something night before last. She'd been sitting on the edge of the bluff drinking a cup of tea, watching the northern lights, when she heard two men shouting on the beach below. Someone fired a gun. From the sharp, cracking sound, she suspected it was a .38 pistol. When she peered over the edge of the cliff, one man had fallen to the ground, and the other guy was running away.

A short time later, the man who had run off came back and picked up the guy lying on the beach, threw him over his shoulder, and staggered away, disappearing around a bend in the shoreline.

Sharon had no way of knowing if either one of these guys ended up in the fish net. And she didn't see any reason why she should get mixed up in someone else's trouble. She'd leave the law to figure it out.

Too exhausted to eat, she lit a small fire in a clearing near the edge of the cliff and brewed a cup of tea. She crawled into her shack, pulled a ragged blanket over her shoulders, and sipped the warm beverage until the cup was empty and she could no longer keep her eyes open.

The wind howled through the cracks in the makeshift walls, a lonely sound that made the ground seem harder than usual. Several hours later, the pack of dogs that came by every night on a hunting foray whined and barked as they nosed around her shanty's door.

She kicked at the flimsy entrance to her shelter. "Beat it," she shouted.

The animals didn't frighten her, they were just annoying. She knew later that night she'd hear the mother moose and her calf walk past her place, chomping at the underbrush as they worked their way along the well-worn trail.

The next day, Sheriff Allen showed up again at the weight station, still wearing his shades even though the sky hung thick with low, dark clouds. Sharon wondered if he thought they made him look like a tough guy in the movies. Though the only thing they did, as far as she was concerned, was probably intimidate a few weak-minded locals and make him look stupid.

"So, where do you live?" Sheriff Allen asked Sharon.

"Up the road."

"Yeah? Now, isn't that a coincidence. I live up the road, too."

Sharon ignored his comment and pulled on her rubber boots.

"I took a long walk on the beach last night," the sheriff said. "Not far from where we suspect this body might have been dragged into the water. It's about a mile from here. I thought I saw the glow of a campfire up on the bluff." He took out a pack of cigarettes, offered one to Sharon.

"Don't smoke," she said.

"So, you know about anyone living up there? You living up the road and all."

"Don't know a thing," Sharon said.

A pickup truck loaded with fish pulled into the weigh station.

"Gotta get kicking." Sharon headed for the truck.

A grubby full-bearded man climbed out of the truck. Two small children, a boy and girl, tumbled out of the front seat and ran close behind the man.

Herb sat in the seat of the forklift, smoking a cigarette. He took a couple more drags then crushed the butt against one of the metal braces of the vehicle before turning the key in the ignition. The forklift coughed a bit of exhaust fumes when Herb tromped a heavy foot on the gas pedal. Sheriff Allen stepped to one side while Sharon stood by the pickup, watching Herb jockey the wooden crate into place with the forklift.

Willie got up from his desk and walked to the pickup. "How's it going?" the bearded man asked Willie.

"Same ol', same ol'," Willie responded.

"You hear about the guy they found in Pete Clauson's net yesterday?" the bearded guy asked.

"I heard," Willie said. "Anyone you know?"

"Don't think so. He wasn't in the water long, but the wildlife down there did a number on his mug. Hard to tell who the guy was."

Herb was having a lot of trouble with the forklift. His eyes were glassy, his skin a sickly ash color. Sharon recognized the drunkard in the young man. She'd been there plenty of times herself.

While she waited for Herb to get the crate situated by the tailgate of the pickup, her gaze followed the little boy and girl as they investigated the horseshoe pit on the other side of the weigh station. This particular fisherman regularly brought loads of fish to Willie's, but he'd never dragged his kids along with him before. Sharon smiled at the sight of the children playing and wondered if her daughter would ever forgive her for deserting the family. Sharon's mother, furious that social services had taken the little girl away, was granted custody and refused to have anything to do with Sharon. It all seemed like such a long time ago.

Bright sunlight broke through the thick clouds and played in the little girl's dark hair, reflecting off the fish scales that dotted the child's ponytail, sparkling as if she were draped in jewels.

"What the hell's the matter with you, Herb? Get that box in place," Willie shouted.

"I'm trying!" Herb bellowed. Then with one more backward and forward motion, Herb managed to align the crate with the bed of the truck.

"You're hanging out too late at night. If you can't do the job right, I'll get someone who can."

"Forget it," Herb growled.

"Not with all the money you owe me."

The father and son were always squabbling. Sharon knew that if Herb had a choice, he wouldn't have been living with his parents. As far as she could figure out from the scraps of angry conversation she'd overheard, Herb had tried to make it on his own in Anchorage, but something happened and he came home this summer, his tail tucked between his legs. Willie had raised a cocky son, and there was nothing he could do about it now.

Willie's wife never came into the weigh station, and the woman never left the house, at least not during the work day. Family business could get complicated, Sharon knew that first hand, and Willie sounded like he might have been battling with everyone in his household. Sharon didn't need to get involved with the old coot's family troubles. She only wanted the pay that was owed her, a dry place to sleep, and to be left alone.

She jumped onto the bed of the truck and sloshed around atop the mound of fish until she'd emptied the load of salmon into the crate.

When she'd kicked the last fish off the truck, Sheriff Allen walked over to her. "Leave me alone," she mumbled.

"So, you in a better mood to talk now?" he asked.

Sharon jumped off the back of the truck. "I smell the same, don't I?"

"Probably," Allen replied.

"Well, my mood's kind of unpleasant, too, about the same as my smell."

Herb slipped the tongs of the forklift under the crate full of fish, but he jammed the gears into reverse too quickly. The vehicle rocked sideways, and the crate toppled over, scattering salmon across the concrete floor.

"Shit!" Willie shouted. "What's wrong with you, boy?"

Herb jumped off the forklift. "Go to hell!" He stomped out of the building and climbed onto his Harley. He revved up the engine, raced down the gravel road heading for the highway, leaving the mess for everyone else to clear up.

"That boy giving you trouble, Willie?" the sheriff asked.

"Since he came back from Anchorage, I haven't had a moment's peace. If it's not his loud music, it's that damn motorcycle. He's out all night, and the damned fool can't do anything right. I'm afraid he's a hopeless case. His mother won't hear a word of criticism about him and gives the kid money behind my back. Too bad we can't lock his ass up in your jail house and see if that would knock some sense into his thick skull."

"Sorry, Willie, I don't get involved with domestic situations unless one of you happens to beat on the other." Sheriff Allen removed his glasses and wiped a bit of slime that had splashed on his face.

"It might come to that," Willie grumbled.

"I'm going to pretend I didn't hear what you just said, Willie."

"What about my fish?" the bearded man called out. "I can't wait around all day to get my load weighed."

Willie, Sharon, and the bearded man righted the crate. The little girl and her brother lifted a twelve-pound Sockeye, one child at each end of the slippery thing. Standing on tiptoes, the children grunted and huffed until they finally shoved the fish over the edge and into the crate.

Willie drove the forklift for the remainder of the afternoon. Herb still hadn't shown up by quitting time.

There was a distinct chill in the air as Sharon walked through the woods to her encampment. She'd lived in Alaska all her life and knew the seasons could change on a dime, and she figured that there might be one more week of work at the weigh station. Willie hadn't said when he thought the net fishing season would be over, but a couple of part-timers who worked for Willie from time to time told her they'd planned to pull up stakes in a day or two.

Sharon wound her way along the narrow path to her camp, looking forward to a bit of food, some quiet. She halted in dismay as she entered the tiny clearing and cursed. The place was totally trashed. The walls of the rickety shack lay atop each other in such a mess that her meager home looked like a garbage heap.

At first, she thought a moose had gone on a rampage and kicked her living quarters to shambles. She looked for hoof tracks but found only boot treads on one of the sheets of plywood. The corrugated roof, dragged to the edge of the bluff, now sat teetering in the wind. No animal had done this.

The cooler had been pulled down from the tree, the lid torn off, its contents scattered among the underbrush. Her few possessions from a life she barely remembered were stomped and broken. The only photo of Tasha, her daughter, rested face down in the mud. Sharon cleaned the image of the little girl as best she could, but a long crack in the surface of the paper cut the innocent smile in half.

A nearly empty peanut butter jar sat under a bush, the lid nowhere in sight. A skimpy trail of ants crawled about in the gooey mess. "I'll bet you guys think you hit a jackpot," she said and scooped the mess of bugs from her food.

Every tea bag from the box had been ground into the earth by a heavy boot heel.

Sharon set the walls of the structure back into place and dragged the sheet of corrugated metal back onto the top of the structure. She wondered if it would be wise for her to crawl inside the thing tonight.

What if the vandals came back?

Even the ragged blanket she slept in was nowhere in sight. She'd spent worse nights out in the open. One thing about being a drunk in this country, you learned to sleep where you passed out. Many mornings she'd awakened surprised at how the night had comforted her.

It didn't take her long to realize there was no way she could spend another night in the shelter, and she explored the area around her campsite looking for a soft place to settle in for the night. When she found a suitable location, she gathered handfuls of branches, mulch, and other forest debris and quickly wove a makeshift blanket. She sat down on the moss, leaned against the tree trunk, and pulled the stiff branch cover up over her shoulders.

The sun eventually settled behind the ridge of mountains on the other side of Cook Inlet, and a pale purple hue filled the sky. Night would take over the land eventually, but until then, the dim glow of the setting sun would last for hours.

Sharon leaned her head against the tree, knowing that she could not fall completely asleep. She closed her eyes and drifted into a semi-wakeful state, something she'd learned from her grandfather who taught her how the old-time trappers used to survive in the wild.

In the stillness of the night, an image crossed her mind of the little sister and brother carrying the heavy fish. She smiled. They were such serious, little workers. Her thoughts shifted to her own daughter and wondered if in the night she cried for a mother.

The soft swooshing sound of an owl's wings startled Sharon to attention as the bird landed on a tree limb nearby. The night passed quietly, softly, until the roar of a motorcycle engine in the distance disturbed the silence. It came closer, until a single beam of light ripped through the underbrush. The machine was traveling up the moose trail, coming straight toward her camp.

Sharon lowered herself deeper into her covering. The driver of the cycle stopped and then positioned his headlight to shine on the shack. The sound of heavy boots tromped across the ground, cracking twigs, moving with a clumsy, awkward gait. Clearly, the person was a stranger to the wilderness. The driver came into the light of his own vehicle. Herb pulled off his riding goggles and kicked at the side of the shack.

"I hate the smell of you, fish kicker," he shouted. With a heavy boot, he pushed roughly at the wall. It easily slid to the ground.

Sharon breathed soft and slow as Herb stomped on the rickety structure. Then with the angry eyes of a man gone mad, he looked down at what he had done. He walked to his bike and turned the front wheel from side to side, casting the headlight across the underbrush. The light slid past the spot where Sharon hid. She closed her eyes to keep her pupils from reflecting in the glare.

He revved his engine several times. "I know you're out there, fish kicker! It'll be safer if you just go back to where you came from."

He let out a howl like a triumphant warrior and then spit into the darkness. The man turned the bike around and drove back along the moose trail, making his way to the highway.

Herb didn't frighten her; the idiot was too much of a fool to be feared.

She remained in her hiding place the rest of the night, and at first light, she crawled out, dusted herself off, and walked along the edge of the bluff, pushing her way through the underbrush to the weigh station.

She'd decided to hit the road and sat near the horseshoe pit waiting for Willie to arrive. More cash would be useful, but after last night, not even the steady pay could keep her hanging around any longer. She'd miss the convenience of the small toilet facility to wash up each day and take care of her meager laundry, though. Herb was just too crazy. It was time to move on.

"You're early," Willie said as he passed her on his way to the weigh station entrance. "I didn't know you liked your work that much."

"I don't," Sharon said. "Today's my last day. I'll collect my pay after the last pickup drops its load."

Willie didn't seem surprised. He shrugged. "Okay."

Sharon glanced at the Harley parked near the house. "Did Herb come back last night?"

"God knows when."

Herb didn't come out of the house until after the noon break, and then when he did show his face, instead of working, he sat on the ground, polishing the wheel rims of the bike. At one point, Sharon caught him watching her. His eyes were mean, angry, threatening.

Willie did not say a word to his son and drove the forklift himself. He gave Sharon a few extra tasks, jobs Herb would have ordinarily done. Tomorrow, Willie would have to manage on his own. How this thing worked out between father and son wasn't any concern of hers.

It didn't surprise Sharon when, later that afternoon, the sheriff's car drove up the road. He'd stopped at the weigh station every day since the body had been caught in the fishnet. She suspected he was going to ask her the same nonsensical questions, but this time, he walked directly to Willie.

Sheriff Allen took off his sunglasses. "I hear net fishing season's almost over."

"That's what they tell me," Willie responded. "You find any more bodies floating around in the water?" He picked a few fish scales off the back of his hand.

"No more bodies. We found out who he was though, a guy by the name of Butch Benton, from Anchorage. Seems like he'd done a good deal of jail time. Had his prints on file."

"Well, you've been busy, now haven't you?" Willie rubbed his hands together. A cool breeze blew into the weigh station.

Sharon stood in the doorway. The sheriff glanced over at her. "How you doing today?"

"Fine," she said.

Sheriff Allen glanced around the shed. "Butch was last seen at the Irish Eyes Tavern. Someone said they saw him leave the bar with Herb. And they never saw him again, left his beer on the bar and his motorcycle in the parking lot."

Willie didn't respond.

"Willie, you own a .38?"

"I own a few guns. Doesn't everyone around here?"

Sharon couldn't tell if suspicion or anger raced across Willie's face, but he looked like he might have been holding his breath, waiting for the sheriff to say more.

"Herb own one, too?" The sheriff watched Herb polishing his Harley.

"What are you getting at, Allen?"

"I think I'll have a chat with Herb." Sheriff Allen turned and walked out into the sunlight. He passed the horseshoe pit and stopped behind Herb.

The color drained from Willie's face, and Sharon realized that he most likely suspected all along what his son had been up to.

The sheriff said something to Herb before putting a hand on the biker's shoulder. Herb leaped up and started running toward the edge of the bluff. Sheriff Allen didn't look like much of an athlete, but he outran Herb. Grabbing him by the collar, the sheriff pulled the young man down to the ground.

"Oh, God," Willie gasped.

Sharon winced. Fear struck the tired old fishmonger's face as if he'd been hit in the gut with a club.

"I'm sorry about this, Willie," Sheriff Allen said, and handcuffed Herb and escorted him to the patrol car. "Maybe it'll all work out, but I got to take your boy in."

Herb no longer resisted and willingly climbed into the back seat of the patrol car. When the sheriff made a U-turn and was driving out toward the main road, Herb gave his father a smile that more resembled a sneer.

Willie sighed heavily, and the poor old man looked smaller, frailer, as though half of his life had drained from his body. He closed the doors of the shed. "Wait here," he said. "I'll bring your money." The words trembled in the old man's throat.

Sharon slipped off the smelly rubber boots, leaning them against the door. She felt sorry for Willie. He hadn't done badly by her.

A few minutes later, the screen door to the back porch of the house slammed shut. Willie walked toward her and handed her an envelope. "Thanks," he said.

Sharon did not count the money. She nodded, shoved the envelope into her pocket, and walked down the gravel road. This time when she reached the highway, she turned right, not left. She had the picture of her daughter in her pocket, and though she'd tried to clean up the campsite so that it didn't look so much like a heap of garbage, she'd taken nothing else with her. Everything back there amounted to trash.

She had walked several miles when Sheriff Allen drove by. He parked his vehicle in front of her and stepped out, still wearing those stupid shades. "Where you headed?" he asked.

"You tell me."

"I have no idea where you're going, fish kicker."

"Sharon. My name's Sharon Wolf."

"Well, Ms. Wolf, it's going to get pretty cold out here soon. I brought you something." He opened the back door to his patrol car and took out a heavy winter coat and handed it to her. "Thought you could use it."

She took the coat, nodded, but said nothing.

"Maybe we'll see you again next fish-kicking season."

"Maybe."

Sheriff Allen got back into his car and sped off down the road.

Heavy dark clouds floated in from the inlet and hung close to the earth. A whistling wind blew a sharp breeze into Sharon's ears. She put on the coat the sheriff had given her and wondered if any one had bothered to come by her mother's place to chop enough firewood for the old woman's winter stash.

Chapter Two

THE DAYS GREW SHORTER, THE nights miserably cold, after Sharon left Willie's weigh station. She traveled on foot for almost a month, zigzagging across the Kenai Peninsula, trying to decide what she was going to do. Heading off in the direction of Anchorage, she doubled back to Kenai. Another time, she thought about traveling south to Juneau but returned again to Kenai. Once, she'd gotten halfway to Cooper Landing, where her mother lived, thinking she'd try to see her daughter, but lost courage and went off in another direction. Her feet felt like they were starting to wear out though she wasn't getting very far.

She traveled back and forth along the same roads and knew that the people in the area probably recognized her even if they didn't know her name. A couple of times, she ran into Willie, once in Kenai at the new mega shopping center and another time at a gas station on a back road up north. He was polite, friendly, and even offered her a ride. But she declined his offer, said she was heading in the opposite direction, and he went on his way. Neither one of them mentioned Herb.

The sheriff's car drove past her several times, usually in hot pursuit and never stopped to talk with her again. But she knew that the Kenai Sheriff Department covered a large section of this part of the state and she figured that wherever she settled in for the winter, Sheriff Allen would probably have jurisdiction over that area.

The road was a lonely place. On long stretches between towns, she'd see maybe one or two cars in an hour. When she got closer to a mom and pop's or a bar stuck out in the boondocks, she'd see a few more vehicles. She never failed to brace herself every time a motor-cycle roared up from behind, thinking it might be Herb seeking her out. A gas station attendant had told her Herb had been let go. He didn't know why, just said that he'd sold him a carton of cigarettes a few weeks back.

But she had other things to deal with. When winter hit, it would be impossible to sleep in the underbrush. She made up her mind to settle down in the next town that she came to.

The weather this time of the year, before the snow, turned wet and cold. And the last couple of nights, she'd been awakened by small earthquakes. Tremors were common in Alaska, though after the one last night, the trees danced for quite a while even after the earth quieted down. Her money was getting low, too. She kept a pretty tight hold on the cash in her pocket and hadn't eaten much more than bags of chips in the last couple of days. Her stomach was growling like a she-bear.

There had been a low cloud cover all day, and by the dampness in the air, there'd be rain again before nightfall. It had already rained plenty, soaking her to the bone several times since she'd hit the road. She didn't know how much more being wet and cold she could take.

Several cars and a pickup truck loaded down with firewood whizzed past, just before a pack of dogs, one missing a hind leg, ran cross the road in front of her. The lead dog sniffed the air, gave her the once over, and then scrambled into the underbrush.

She'd been on this road several times before. The stream of smoke up ahead was coming from a gas station in a community not much bigger than a turn-around on a shoulder of the highway. There was a gas station on one side of the road and a scruffy-looking bar, The Nowhere, on the other side with its flickering partially burned-out neon sign.

By the time she reached the gas station, the cloud cover had drifted so low to the earth that it absorbed all worldly sound except for the flapping American Legion and P.O.W. flags hanging out front. The Nowhere was open for business with cars and pickup trucks parked along one side of the building. The pickup loaded down with firewood that passed her earlier stood idling at the gas pump, a yelping dog on the driver's seat.

Sharon opened the door to the gas station. The smell of burned coffee hung in the air. She'd been in this place before and recognized the bearded man perched on a stool behind the counter. Sometimes his wife, a large-boned woman with a thick black braid that hung down to her waist, sat inside the store while her husband worked the gas pumps. Once, a teenager, a pretty girl with long straight hair, sat on the floor brushing the fur of the most beautiful Siberian Husky Sharon had ever seen. Today, the shop owner was alone. He nodded a welcome, but his suspicious eyes followed Sharon as she stepped in front of the coffee machine.

"We got fresh sandwiches," he said.

"What kind?"

"The wife made egg salad and tuna today."

"I'll take tuna." Sharon poured coffee into a mug. She dug deep into her pocket for some cash, carefully fingering the money so that she'd only pull out one bill. No need to let anyone know that she'd shoved every last cent she owned down in her pocket.

"That'll be two-fifty," he said.

She handed him a five and cradled the hot cup of coffee in her cold hands, waiting for change. Several battered chrome kitchen chairs, their plastic seats repaired with duct tape, sat in front of a blazing wood-burning stove.

"Mind if I sit over there and eat?" she asked.

"Be my guest."

Sharon didn't know what pleased her the most at this moment: the food, sitting in a chair, or being warm. They all wanted to be first on the list, but she had to admit that the food was the most satisfying.

The door to the mini mart swung open, and a wiry little guy stuck his head in. "Phil, throw me a pack of cigs. I got to drop off a load of fire wood across the street."

A red pack of cigarettes flew across the room.

"Thanks. I'll catch you later when Johnny pays me."

Sharon took a drink of her coffee, her back to the door.

"Hey, didn't I pass you on the road? If I'd known you were a woman, I'd of given you a ride. Where'd you come from?"

"Benny, just go deliver that fire wood. Mind your own business," Phil said.

"Right. Right, later." Benny headed out to his truck.

Sharon finished her coffee, ate the sandwich, and sat in front of the fire a short while longer.

"I'm going to make a fresh pot of coffee. You want more?" Phil said.

"If it's not too much trouble."

Sharon went to the candy counter and picked out a chocolate crunch bar. After pouring herself another cup of the brew, she dug down into her pocket for more money.

"This one's on me," Phil said.

Sharon nodded, returned to her seat, and unwrapped the candy bar. She didn't usually take charity, but her cash was getting too dangerously low to refuse.

"It's started," Phil said.

"What?"

"Raining."

Sharon looked out the window and watched as large raindrops struck the few remaining leaves on a black cottonwood tree.

"How far you headed?" Phil asked.

Sharon shoved the last bit of chocolate into her mouth, crumpled up the empty candy wrapper. "Quite a ways," she said.

"Did your car break down?"

"Got none."

"What do you reckon you're going to do?"

Sharon felt a bit drunk from the food and the warmth of the stove. She turned and looked at Phil. "Got no plans."

"If you're going to stick around for a while, they could use some help in the bar across the road. The keeper's wife got herself banged up in a car wreck the other night. She used to take care of the kitchen. You could go over and see what they say. Ask for Johnny. Tell him Phil sent you."

"Thanks, I'll do that." Sharon put on her coat.

The wind had started to blow, the temperature dropped, and the rain, now turned to sleet, made shrill pinging sounds as the ice crystals hit the pavement. Benny's pickup was parked in front of the bar, and he carried the last armload of wood into the bar. The dog sitting in the front seat barked furiously as Sharon walked past the truck.

The bar was a lot bigger on the inside than it looked from the road and quite a bit cooler compared to the mini market. Two dirty windows at the far end of the place scarcely let in any light. The walls, a mix of rough-cut timber and fake wood paneling, were covered with trophy heads of everything from long horned mountain goats to moose with black marble eyes. A large mirrored wall behind the cash register reflected each animal head as if they had a twin. In one corner, a stuffed bear, a little taller than an average-sized man, stood menacingly with outstretched paws and displaying a full set of canines.

"You Johnny?" Sharon asked the man standing behind the bar.

"I am."

"Phil across the way said you might need some help in the kitchen."

"He's right on that point. The wife will be out of commission for a while with a dislocated shoulder. You interested in working?"

"Yeah."

"Got a problem with starting tonight?"

"No."

"You know how to work a grill?"

"Yes."

"It's simple around here. Burgers and fries most days, sometimes eggs and flapjacks on Sundays, and if you feel like starting up the pressure cooker, you could offer fried chicken. The wife was afraid of the thing. That'd be up to you."

"I worked one of them a while back."

"Good. Take a look at the place and see what you think. I'll pay you the minimum wage to start."

"The pay is fine," she said. "I can't say how long I'll be staying."

"I'm not asking for a relationship. All I need is a fry cook. It doesn't matter for how long."

The upper half of one wall had been broken through from the bar to the kitchen and a waist-high counter built to give the cook somewhere to put the food for the customer to grab. This wasn't a place for waitress service, and Sharon wondered if there hadn't been a cook in the kitchen, would the truck drivers and locals who stopped by for a beer be expected to cook their own burgers? She turned the light on and saw right away from yellow grease stains on the walls that the kitchen needed a good cleaning.

Sharon opened the freezer door. On one side of the compartment were dozens of burger patties neatly stacked and ready to be cooked. Next to the patties were buns piled every which way, and though they took up a great deal of room, it seemed a good way to store them without having to deal with moldy buns.

Lettuce and tomatoes were not easy to keep fresh this far from the major shipping ports so Sharon didn't even bother to look for them. On the other hand, onions were the most popular addition to the Alaskan burger, and a huge gunnysack of them stood in one corner of the room. It looked to Sharon like those onions had been there for quite some time. Green shoots poked out of the bottom of the bag looking more like a spring planting than a winter supply. Several gallon jars of dill pickles, sweet relish, along with giant containers of spices, and bottles of ketchup were lined up on a shelf near the back door.

Sharon bent close to the grill and took a whiff. The griddle, covered in a thick layer of cooked-on grease, smelled of rancid oil. She rolled up her sleeves and set out to scrub down the place before she even attempted to turn on the grill. The afternoon passed quickly as she emptied the grease bin, scraped down the grill, drained the fryer, and replaced it with fresh oil.

After taking a small batch of frozen meat patties and a couple packs of buns from the freezer, she sliced a batch of onions. She wiped the last of the tears from her eyes.

A woman called out to her from the doorway, "Where'd you come from?"

Sharon looked up at the woman but said nothing.

"I'm Julie. I own this place. Who the hell are you?"

"I'm your new fry cook," Sharon said.

"Good, you can have the damned job," Julie said. "Seems like you might know what you're doing by the looks of the place so far."

Julie leaned against the doorsill, one arm secured in a sling. She rubbed her elbow. "You here for the night or will you be hanging around for a while?"

"Don't know yet."

Julie looked quizzically at her. "Got a name?"

"Sharon."

"Where you staying?"

Sharon shrugged, realizing that it must look pretty obvious that she'd been on the road.

"Thought so," Julie said. "We've got a bed in the back room. We use it to stow the guys who can't walk a straight line. I'll tell Johnny the room's off limits if you're interested in sticking around for a while."

"Thanks." Sharon nodded.

The front door to the bar opened, and someone called out, "Hey, Julie, how you doing?"

She waved with her good arm.

A cool breeze eased across the floor. Sharon looked down at her feet.

"That happens every time someone comes into the place. Watch that it doesn't blow out the pilot light on the fryer. It's happened before. Filled the place with fumes one night and would have blown the building to kingdom come if one of the regulars hadn't been sleeping in the back room. That's why I put aluminum foil across the front of the knobs. Keeps the possibility down to a minimum. But it wouldn't be any big loss if this sorry ass joint was blown off the map."

Johnny stuck his head into the kitchen. "I see you gals have met." He kissed Julie on the top of her head. "How you doing, baby?"

"Keep the drunk crowd out of the back room," she said and pulled away from him. "Sharon's going to bed down in there for a while."

"Right, boss." Johnny grabbed his wife and gave her a rather gruff hug. "How about this woman? Yesterday she rolled her pickup truck, crawled out on her own, walked back to town, and here she is standing in the kitchen, not even twenty-four hours later, giving me orders. Baby, you are just too precious." He forced a kiss on her cheek, gave her a pat on the butt, and then looked at Sharon. "Turn on the grill. You got your first order for the night. Two burgers with everything and a double order of fries."

Julie pulled away from her husband. "A regular order of fries is two handfuls of frozen potatoes," she said and walked out of the kitchen.

Sharon flipped a steady stream of burgers that first night. A few folks hung around, leaning on the counter, chitchatting. Most were curious about the new fry cook; though several guys were so drunk they had no idea what they were saying. One old geezer offered Sharon a ride to see his house on the lake. Then he nearly fell flat on his face, tripping on his own pointed-toe cowboy boots as he headed back to the barstool where he'd been sitting all night, throwing back beers.

An unexpected treat was the selection of music in the jukebox. Sharon hadn't heard some of those songs since she was a little girl, old two-step tunes she remembered her mother and father singing years ago. Sharon hummed along, flipping burgers and lightly tapping her foot in time with the music. She'd forgotten how quickly time passed when she listened to music. The night seemed young, and she felt as though she could go on cooking burgers for hours.

The grimy clock above the sink told a different tale. It was well onto one o'clock in the morning when Julie came back into the kitchen. "We're closing up. Let me show you where you'll be sleeping. It's nothing fancy, but it's warm."

Sharon followed Julie out into the bar. A lone couple on the dance floor hung onto each other, swaying to an oldie about blue eyes and rain.

"Come on, folks, break it up. Take it home, will ya," Julie called out to the dancers.

Johnny stood behind the bar, wiping down the counter. "You heard the little lady," he said. "That's the last song. The night's over."

Julie led Sharon down a short corridor and opened the door to a room that wasn't much larger than a storage closet with one small window. The walls were cracked, and the sheet rock in one corner of the wall facing the woods looked like someone had rammed a fist through, trying to grab a branch of the tree outside the window. There was a camper's cot for a bed, a lamp on a rickety wooden crate turned upside down, and nothing else.

"No one will come back to the bar until late tomorrow afternoon," Julie said. "On weekends, we open the grill during the day, but you don't need to know the schedule. We'll discuss it later if you're still interested in staying. Just put things away and turn the stove off. I'm going home. And for your information, we keep a close watch on the booze so don't help yourself."

Sharon hadn't slept in a bed in over a year, and at that moment, she fought a strong urge to fall onto the cot. Instead, she went back out into the kitchen to finish cleaning up.

"I suppose we'll see you later," Johnny said as he stuck his head into the kitchen.

"Suppose so," Sharon replied.

"Good night." Johnny's voice sounded heavy and tired. "Turn out the lights after we've gone."

Julie went out the front door.

"Wait up, baby," Johnny called to his wife. "I'll drive you home."

"Go to hell," Julie shouted. "I wouldn't ride with you if you were the last man standing."

"Ah, come on. Let's call a truce."

"Over my dead body," she snapped. "Go crawl in bed with someone else. I've had it with you."

"Whatever," Johnny said. "That arm of yours is no damn good for driving, and you're going to end up in another ditch. You might not be so lucky this time."

"Don't be so dramatic," Julie said and slammed the car door.

The cold air sent the couple's angry words through the walls of the bar as though a telephone wire connected them directly to the kitchen. Sharon heard one of the car engines start up, and the driver revved the motor. The second car cranked to a start. Then the cars drove off, each in a different direction.

The place became desperately quiet when Sharon turned out the lights. Fatigue hit her like a heavy burden. She went into the back room to the rickety cot and, in one blissful moment, slipped into a deep sleep. There were no dreams, no uneasy disturbances, and no regrets. There was only nothingness.

This time of the year the daylight didn't show up until well into the mid morning hours, and when Sharon next opened her eyes, the thin curtain hanging over the east-facing window of the little bedroom couldn't keep out the sun that glared through the dirty glass panes. Someone walked past her door. She quickly got up and stepped out of her room. "Who's there?" she called.

"Morning," Benny said. "Hope I didn't disturb you." "

What are you doing here?"

"I clean up the place and take out the empties from the night before."

"How'd you get in?"

"I got a key to the back door. I brought an extra coffee. Want it?"

Sharon rubbed the back of her neck. "Yeah, I could use some." She sat down on one of the bar stools.

He handed her the hot coffee. "Where'd you come from?"

Sharon didn't say anything.

"You're not from around here," Benny persisted.

"You ask too many questions."

"I don't mean anything by it, just curious."

"I got nothing to hide, but I don't answer questions."

"Fair enough."

Benny dragged the box of empty beer bottles out from behind the bar. He ducked down under the counter and came up with a few more bottles that had rolled out of Johnny's reach the night before. He set them on top of the box. "Old beer has a strong smell in the morning, don't you think?"

"Yep." Sharon took another drink of coffee.

"Want some whiskey in that brew?"

"No, I like my coffee just like this."

"Suit yourself." Benny poured a hefty shot into his coffee. "Gives me a kick start."

"Yeah, I know," said Sharon.

Benny settled himself several barstools away from Sharon. He took a healthy swallow of his coffee and then took out a pack of cigarettes. "Suppose you don't smoke."

"That habit's gotten too rich for my pocketbook."

Benny nodded in agreement and sucked in a deep lungful of the smoke. He fidgeted for a while on the bar stool, swallowed the last of his brew, and flicked a long ash into the empty paper cup. "Well, I got to go." He cleared his throat and smashed the cigarette against the inside of the cup. "Nice talking to you," he said, then lifted the box of empties and headed for the back door. Just before the door slammed shut, Benny's voice drifted to her. "I left you some breakfast out here in the kitchen."

She leaned one elbow on the counter and swallowed a bit more of the coffee. The acrid smell of burning paper alerted her to the fact Benny's coffee cup had caught fire. After grabbing the smoldering cup, she dowsed it in the sink behind the counter.

Chapter Three

THE MORNING AIR WAS DAMP and cold. A chill crept across Sharon's shoulders, and she stuck several logs into the wood stove.

Sleeping on the ground for the last year had certainly toughened her spirit, though she thought that the hard earthen mattress and sleepless nights she'd spent keeping vigil over her decrepit shanty had aged her bones. The dampness in the air with the approaching winter season made her back ache, and she moved closer to the stove.

She finished her coffee and threw the paper cup into the fire. The place looked larger in the morning light than it had yesterday, and except for the animal heads decorating the walls, the bar offered little in the way of character. But then, no one asked for much more than the simplest of creature comforts and a steady flow of booze when they came to a joint like The Nowhere.

The rough timber walls snapped and clicked as the room warmed up. A scruffy moose head on the far wall appeared to stare straight down at her. Its glass eyes caught the light in a way that made the old thing look like it was smirking.

"What are you looking at?" she grumbled. She went into the ladies' room where she washed herself with a wad of paper towels. She'd done this so often in the last year that it seemed natural. The toilet in the weigh station didn't have the greatest facility, but it was better than nothing. And since she'd left Willie's, every time she came to a gas station, she headed for the bathroom to freshen up. Washing her hair had been the most difficult, and if she'd have been taller, it might have been an easier task. In the end, getting clean always felt like a burden had been lifted from her shoulders.

Sharon stood near the woodstove, combing her wet hair. A year ago in a drunken rage, she'd whacked her hair off nearly to her ears. It had grown some but still looked pretty jagged. And she thought she'd never get rid of the fish scales that got tangled in her hair while she worked at the weigh station.

The crackling of the wood burning in the stove was a lonely sound. Digging down into the pocket of her jeans, she pulled out a few coins and walked to the jukebox. Just about every song on the play list was familiar. She dropped the coins into the slot, selected a few songs, then went back to the woodstove and continued drying her hair.

The first song was a tune someone played last night, a heartbreaker she remembered her mother singing. So much had happened since the days when her mother sang every night, and she couldn't tell if listening to the song made her happy or sad. She closed her eyes and saw her mother again as a young woman, trim and hearty, sitting in front of the potbelly stove singing, encouraging Sharon and her brothers to join in. They'd even performed as a family at local community picnics. That was before her father was killed in a logging accident. After that, everything changed.

Sharon sang along with the next tune and marveled that she remembered the words after all these years even though her voice sounded craggy and weak. It felt like her throat was coated with a thick pasty mess. She stayed on key even with her cracking voice. When the jukebox lifted its mechanical arm to bring up another record, Sharon coughed and tried to clear her vocal chords the best she could before the music started up again.

She sang the words of the next song with the familiarity of meeting an old friend, each line and every pause in the melody solidly ingrained in her mind. Her throat felt tight, strained, but she continued singing, remembering how much pleasure she used to get from music.

There were only a few coins left in her pocket, and when the jukebox stopped playing, she felt sadly empty, something she hadn't felt before the music started. Reaching into her pocket, hoping she'd overlooked a quarter, she was disappointed to find none. She sighed and once again dragged the comb through her hair.

The windows at the far end of the bar, even as dirty as they were, glowed with a burst of light from the midday sunshine. The bottles lined up on one wall of the bar caught the light, and the booze gleamed amber, tan and dazzling clear. One container glowed a vibrant jade green. The whisky bottle still sat on the counter where Benny left it. Sharon's mouth filled with saliva, and an old familiar feeling came back to her. She clenched her jaw and stood perfectly still, watching dust particles float across a shaft of sunlight.

"Damn. It's never going to stop." She turned her back to the bar, went into the kitchen, and was scrubbing the wall behind the grill when a breeze blew across her feet.

"How you doing?" Phil called from across the room.

"Just fine."

"Thought I'd stop by, see if you needed anything." Phil stepped into the kitchen, a grocery bag cradled in one arm. "I brought you a few supplies. How'd you like an elk steak for lunch? And here are some eggs. There's usually not much in this place to eat but burgers." Phil emptied the contents of the bag onto the counter.

"Thank you," Sharon said. "Let me pay you for this." She stuck her hand into her pocket.

"No, this is on me. I'm on my way to Anchorage. I have to pick up a load of supplies. Beverly will look after the store while I'm away. If there's anything you need, just go over and tell her." Phil patted the slab of meat. "You might want to slice this up and freeze the rest for another day. Unless you're a coyote, it's a lot of meat to eat in one sitting."

"This is very thoughtful," Sharon said.

"Don't mention it. Remember, if you need anything, just ask Beverly."

Sharon looked down at the meat. "I'm sure going to enjoy this."

"I thought as much. See you in a couple of days." A cold draft traveled across the floor again when Phil opened the door. He turned around and called back into the bar, "The kitchen never looked so good, by the way. But don't tell Julie I said so."

The daylight faded away early in the North Country this time of year. By mid-afternoon, the stream of sunshine that had glowed so brightly earlier no longer filtered through the dirty windows. On the far side of the bar, a grey twilight filled the room. Sharon turned on a couple of lights, and the place looked a little livelier. A short time later, Julie showed up with Johnny dragging in a few minutes later. Neither one of them looked like they'd gotten much sleep though Sharon thought Johnny looked the worst.

"You okay with staying alone in this place?" Johnny asked.

"Yeah, fine," Sharon replied. "Benny came by this morning, and Phil brought a few groceries and an elk steak for my lunch."

"Sounds like you had a busy day. I wasn't sure you'd still be here this evening."

"Suppose I'll stay for a while."

"Good." Julie inserted a key into the cash register and pulled out a small stack of bills. "I'll handle the money tonight."

"That's fine by me," Johnny said. "How's your shoulder?"

"Hurts like hell. I had to sleep propped up on the couch last night. And then that damned dog of yours started howling early this morn-ing. Lord, I wish you could do something with that animal."

"Well, honey," said Johnny. "He's a hunting dog and probably heard a moose tramping around in the back yard."

Julie and Johnny stood behind the bar, their backs turned to each other. Julie kept fiddling with the money in the cash register while Johnny opened and shut cabinet doors. He flipped open a bottle of beer and chugged down almost half the bottle before he lowered it to the counter. He looked at his wife. "You ready to let me come home?"

Julie slammed the cash register drawer shut. "Ask me later." She looked at Sharon standing in the doorway of the kitchen. "Did Phil say when he was leaving to get supplies?"

"He's gone, left earlier this afternoon," Sharon said.

"Hope he remembers to get everything I had on the list."

"Chill out," Johnny said. "He's never forgotten anything in the past."

Julie glowered at him, poured herself a healthy shot of whisky, and went to a far booth where she leafed through a stack of papers in a folder.

Sharon returned to the kitchen with no intentions of getting tangled up in their squabbling. After removing the slab of meat Phil had dropped off earlier, she cut a big chunk and put it on the grill. The aroma of the meat cooking carried with it a delicious memory of a long time ago hunting with her father and brothers. Flipping the steak over, she sang one of the tunes from the jukebox.

"Hey, you sing good," said Benny.

Sharon quickly turned. "Where'd you come from?"

"From the cold world," he said. "Smells like Phil and Beverly shared that old elk with you. I told them you might appreciate something to eat besides burgers."

"Want some?"

"No. Thanks anyway," Benny said. "Julie, how's that shoulder?"

"Don't ask," Julie snarled.

"We're going to leave the princess in the corner to lick her wounds," Johnny said. "The lady wants nothing to do with us tonight. Sharon, that steak smells mighty good. When it's done cooking, bring it out here and join us. We need to get better acquainted."

Sharon flipped her steak over several more times to get it browned on both sides but mindful not to overcook the meat. She'd always been good at preparing food, and so far, this job suited her just fine. Being in the kitchen always made her feel peaceful and happy. She placed the elk steak on a double layer of paper plates and carried it out to where Benny and Johnny sat on bar stools, sucking on beers.

Johnny lifted his beer bottle. "Want one?"

"Nope," she said.

"Damn, that meat smells good," Johnny said. "If I hadn't already eaten, I'd ask for some."

"Which little lovebird cooked for you today?" Julie asked, though she didn't look up. She continued shuffling the envelopes across the table, stacking them in neat piles.

Johnny ignored his wife's insinuation and went behind the bar.

Benny took a swig of his beer. "Did anyone feel that quake last night? My damned place rattled so hard I thought it was going to cave in."

"Didn't feel a thing," Johnny said. "How about you, Sharon? This old bar rock and roll?"

"Can't say I felt anything," Sharon said. She looked at Julie, waiting for her to say something. Julie remained silent, shuffling her papers from one pile to another.

"They say it's old Redoubt getting ready to blow its top." Benny took a swallow of beer. "That volcano is at it again. I heard on the news this morning that the guys who keep tabs on the thing said that the glacier cap cracked yesterday."

Sharon knew Redoubt. The weigh station in Kenai hadn't been but thirty miles across the inlet from the legendary volcano. She'd sat on the bluff quite a few nights, looking out at the mountain range on the other side of Cook Inlet, watching old Redoubt puffing out little clouds of smoke into the sunset.

"You think we'll get any of the ash if it blows?" Benny asked.

"Beats the shit out of me," Johnny said. "And what would you do if we did get some of the ash? It would be useless for you to stay in that old shack of yours. That place is so creaky you'd be sitting in ash up to your ass." Johnny let out a horselaugh at his joke. "Live dangerously, Benny, like the rest of us."

Sharon finished the steak, picked up her plate, and returned to the kitchen. She remembered the last time that mountain blew. Back then, she lived too far south to feel any of the effects. She'd heard it was pretty rough in this area with the dust. Nothing but jagged particles irritated everyone's eyes and throat. Maybe she'd have to rethink wintering in this area. It might be warm holding over in The Nowhere for the winter, but eating volcanic ash didn't appeal to her.

A few people wandered into the place. Someone put money in the jukebox. A little while later, a crowd tramped into the bar, and soon, Sharon had burgers and fries to contend with. After an hour of flipping burgers, the place got real quiet. She braced herself for one of those earthquakes Benny had been talking about, thinking that everyone had felt it but her. Instead, someone began to play an acoustic guitar and sing. He sounded professional, too. She took the last patty off the grill, quickly slapped the burger together, put it on the counter, and went out into the bar to see what was going on.

In one corner, a guy dressed all in black sat in a chair, hunched over a guitar. His toe-tapping tune captivating everyone, and though a couple of guys sitting at the bar took swigs from their bottles of beer, all eyes were on the singer. The musician didn't miss a beat as he strummed the guitar, his Stetson shadowing his face while he looked down at the floor, wailing away.

Sharon moved closer. She knew the song he was singing. Her mother had taught it to her years ago. Sounded like he'd learned his music from the same record her mother had listened to. He stopped singing, fingered a fancy bit of music on the guitar, and then finished off the song with a smooth combination of chords. Lifting his head, he gave the audience a self-satisfied grin. The crowd called out their approval, and then almost to a person, every arm in the place hoisted a drink to their lips.

Johnny handed the singer a bottle of beer.

"Thanks, man." The singer rested one arm on the guitar and threw back the brew as though he were parched. He placed the bottle on the floor, strummed a few slow notes to change the tempo, and looked out at his audience while singing a soft ballad with a two-step beat.

An older couple glided out onto the dance floor and slowly moved to the music. Several men scooted into a booth. One of the men put a deck of playing cards on the table. The conversation in the place picked up a bit. Johnny wiped down the bar counter and opened some beers for a couple of patrons sitting on stools near the draft beer pull handles.

The guitar player sang a few more numbers, not saying a word between his tunes, and he drank every beer Johnny handed him. The guy played to the crowd, and even though he'd caught their attention in the beginning, most everyone came to the bar to either socialize or to get drunk, if they could afford it. He'd played everything from a soppy love song to a few rousing country anthems. And then he stopped playing, put the guitar back into its case, and crawled up onto a barstool. He leaned over and said something to Johnny.

"Hey, Sharon," Johnny called. "Make my friend, Dell, a burger will'ya, and give him an extra order of fries."

Sharon went back into the kitchen and put a patty on the grill. Songs started to run through her mind like remembered old conversations, and she began to hum one of the tunes. She threw the frozen potatoes into the fryer, spread pickle relish on a bun, and topped it with a couple slices of onion. Placing an extra pickle on the dish, she slipped the fries onto a separate paper plate and brought the burger out to the bar.

Dell picked up a few of the fries with the delicate touch of a man still strumming his guitar, and then with one hand, he took up the burger and began to eat as though he hadn't seen food in days. Sharon leaned on one elbow against the counter.

"Why don't you sit for a while," Johnny said. "No one usually orders food this late at night."

Sharon watched Dell eat. After gobbling down a few fries, he no longer used such a delicate touch. It wasn't a pretty sight. He slathered the potatoes with so much ketchup that picking them up individually looked impossible, and he grabbed globs by the handful.

"We usually feed Dell out on the back porch," Johnny said as he took away the empty beer bottle and gave the singer a fresh one.

"I'll come by tomorrow night with Petunia and the little one," Dell said. "The wife's feeling a little under the weather today so she stayed back."

Dell's speech sounded perfectly fine even after all the beers he'd downed, though his eyes looked bloodshot and they had the polished shine of a drunk with one eye wandering a bit to the left.

"You're not from around here," Dell said.

"No," Sharon responded.

"Pushing through?"

"Yeah, something like that." Sharon looked down at the guitar. "You sing well."

"I sing this shit for a few free beers," he said. "Johnny pulled my ass out of the hoosegow a while back and said I could come by and entertain any time I wanted." Dell put the bottle up to his mouth, sucked long and hard on the beer, and brought it back down onto the counter with a hard thud. "You the new fry cook?" He turned around and looked at Julie, who was sitting in the same booth she'd settled into earlier that night. "How do you like working for the dragon lady? She breathe fire on you, yet?"

"That's enough, Dell," Johnny warned. "She's just a bit high strung."

"High strung with a capital B," Dell shot back.

"Don't make me kick you out of here tonight." Johnny took the empty beer bottle from in front of Dell. "You talk nice about my wife, or you say nothing. Got it?"

"You don't have to tell me twice," Dell said.

"I have to tell you every night to mind your manners."

Dell turned his back to Johnny and then leaned toward her. "What's your name?"

"Sharon."

"Well, Sharon, can I buy you one of Johnny's free beers?"

"No." She felt someone leaning over her shoulder.

"Hey, Dell, what's new?" Benny said.

"Nothing's new, Bunny. What's up with you?"

"It's Benny."

"Don't be so touchy. That's what my princess calls you. Bunny's a fine name."

"Whatever," Benny said. "Say, did you feel that earthquake last night?"

"I feel nothing anymore. The ground is always moving under me. When it stops, that's when I'll take notice."

"They say that Redoubt is on the warpath again. Sure as shit, it's going to blow."

"You don't say," Dell said.

"Yeah, it was on the TV this morning."

Dell leaned his back against the counter. "You believe everything you see on the damned boob-tube?"

"No, not everything."

"Take heed, Bunny, my man, they're trying to scare the breeches off your ass. Volcanic ash is nothing but a bit of salt on this earth." Dell put his arm around Benny's shoulder. "If you get too scared, you can come and stay with Petunia and me. That is, if the dog will let you sleep on the couch."

Benny's cheeks flushed, and he looked down at the floor.

Julie got up from her seat. She adjusted her sling and walked toward the bar. "You causing trouble again," she said, looking directing at Dell.

"Me?"

"You're always up to no good."

"You got me all wrong. I'm one of the good guys."

"Bullshit." Julie looked at Johnny and then at Dell. "My husband may have given you a sweetheart deal, but your welcome is just about worn out. You drink and eat more than your worth."

Dell gave Julie a broad grin. "Why, Julie, I'm a gold mine."

"You're a worthless son of a bitch. A quarter will get me the same songs on the jukebox, and I don't have to pour any booze down its throat."

"Who set your tail on fire?"

"You." Julie turned and went into the bathroom.

"Damn, I don't know how Johnny puts up with that woman."

"She's in a lot of pain," Benny said.

"You ask me, she is a pain." Dell stretched and jumped off the barstool. "I think I'll mosey home and see how the old lady is doing. There's always something going on with these women. See you around."

Dell made it only as far as the front door where he stopped to chat with a couple of women hanging out by the jukebox. He leaned in very close to the younger woman, brushed her long blond hair from one shoulder, and whispered something into her ear. She playfully shoved him and laughed. Dell eased himself closer to the pretty young woman, tipping his hat back from his forehead so that he could sidle up even closer.

Chapter Four

PHIL AND BEVERLY CAME BY The Nowhere a couple times a week. They'd each order a burger, sit on barstools, and drink a couple of beers. Beverly usually didn't say much, but one night, she brought a bag of clothes for Sharon. Good stuff, too. From that point on, Sharon gave Beverly a bit more fries with her burger.

After working at the bar for more than a month, Sharon settled into a routine and kept her nose out of Johnny and Julie's personal business.

But Johnny had begun to look poorly, and by the end of some nights when the place emptied out, he was white as a ghost with huge dark circles under his eyes. He took several breaks each night, claiming to need fresh air. He'd lost his appetite and said that even the thought of food made his stomach turn over.

"You got the flu?" Phil asked one night. "Want me to drive you home?"

"No, man, I can manage."

"Give me a holler if you need anything." Phil drank the last of his beer. "Guess we'll be getting home."

Beverly slipped on her coat, adjusted the long dark braid that hung down her back, and followed her husband out the door.

Julie sat in a corner booth, an empty whisky glass in front of her, a fresh cigarette burning in the ashtray, her arm still stuck in a sling. She didn't look up when Phil and Beverly left the bar. Julie didn't complain about any discomfort in the shoulder and never asked for assistance, though Sharon saw her wince from time to time when she moved a certain way. And Julie and Johnny still didn't talk much to each other.

Johnny wiped the last watermark off the counter, folded up the cloth, and walked over to where Julie sat.

She glanced up. "You look like shit." Sharon couldn't hear what Johnny said, but Julie smiled sardonically at Johnny. "Do whatever you want," she said. "Just don't expect me to be your nurse maid."

Johnny went to the cash register and counted out the evening's take.

Sharon eased onto a stool at the bar. She pulled a five-dollar bill from her pocket. "Could you give me change for this?"

"What do you want?"

"Quarters. As many as you can spare."

"Quarters?"

"Yeah, I like to play the jukebox." She'd used all the change she'd squirreled away from the few tips that came her way, and tonight she didn't have a single coin in her pocket.

"No problem." Johnny gave her a fistful of coins.

She handed him the five.

"Keep your money. The music's on me."

Julie pulled on her coat, draped the garment over her injured shoulder, picked up her pack of cigarettes, and left without saying a word.

"I'll be there in a little while," Johnny said.

Julie glared at her husband and opened the door. A howling wind blew into the place, bringing with it a great rush of rain mixed with large sloppy wet snowflakes. Julie shut the door behind her, and the place went deathly silent. For a moment, the wind died down and the weather outside now sounded like nothing more than a mere whisper.

"You sure you can drive?" Benny asked. "You look pretty wobbly."

"I'm going back to my place. Julie's cooled off. I'll be fine." Johnny locked up the cash register.

Though he'd said he was all right, Sharon didn't think he looked well at all. Besides looking so pale, he seemed to have difficulty getting into his coat. Finally, he slipped on a hat and headed for the door.

"This place gets too hot," he complained. "The cold air will perk me up."

Benny trailed out the door behind Johnny. "See you tomorrow," Benny called over his shoulder to Sharon. "Want me to bring you some doughnuts?"

"If you like," Sharon said.

Just before Benny closed the door, the wind picked up again, and a large gust of bad weather burst through the open door, leaving Sharon to mop up the mess. The wind once again beat at the front of the bar, and the door rattled frantically. It felt like the weather was closing in around her. If this was the start of winter, it was going to be one hell of a cold season. She dropped a couple of quarters into the jukebox before going back into the kitchen.

While Sharon put the mop and bucket back into the pantry, the wind let up a bit. She heard scratching at the back door. At first, she thought it was a twig brushing against an outside wall. Then the shrill whining of an animal rose over the wail of the wind. She went to the door, put her ear next to the lock, and listened. It could have been the wind playing tricks. Once she'd heard the wind whimper and cry like an abandoned child.

She turned the lock, opening the door ever so slightly.

On the top step stood a mangy dog. The poor thing raised its head, and the glow of the kitchen spotlighted long open gashes and a deep bite on its snout. The fur on its back, coated in thick lumps of mud and traces of frozen snow, had turned crimson from a bloody wound on its hind end. The whimpering dog stuck its bloody face into the opened doorway. Sharon had seen plenty of dogs that had gone wild. A couple of times, she'd seen one a little too close for comfort, but this mutt didn't frighten her. It might be a free spirit, but it didn't look dangerous. Sharon opened the door all the way, and the dog hobbled into the kitchen. It was the three-legged dog she'd seen a while back crossing the road with the pack of hounds.

Once inside the kitchen, the dog collapsed on the floor. The wounds were deep. The muddy snow on its fur quickly melted, leaving puddles of pink water under the dog's paws.

Sharon only had kitchen detergent to clean the injuries. She went into the pantry, scrounging around for the cleanest rags she could find.

Most animals did not take kindly to being fussed over when they'd been seriously hurt, but the dog let Sharon sop up the bloody wounds with the soapy rag and whimpered only slightly when she picked a twig from inside one of the gouges. She had no medicine to put on the open wounds, but at least they were clean.

After mopping the floor, she threw the dirty water out the back door. In the distance, she heard several dogs call to each other. Then the howling wind blotted out the barking.

She had no idea how far the dog had traveled, but it looked exhausted. "You can't lie next to this drafty door all night." Sharon lifted the animal and carried it into the bar where she put it down next to the wood stove. "That was some nasty fight you got yourself into." She gently petted the top of the dog's head.

Sharon took a few quarters from her pocket and set the jukebox up to play a couple more tunes. She sat down on the floor next to the dog, sighed heavily, and leaned against the wall.

The next thing she knew, Benny was looking down at her.

"Morning, sleeping beauty," he said.

Sharon's shoulders ached, and her ass had gone to sleep. "Shit." She rubbed her neck.

"And where in the hell did you find old Three Toes?" Benny got down on his knees and patted the dog. "Where've you been, old girl? We don't see you around much any more."

"She showed up on the back steps right after you left." Sharon stood, and the dog attempted to stand, too.

"Damn, she took some beating. You put anything on these wounds?"

"I don't have anything," Sharon said.

"I've got a medic kit in my truck." Benny rushed out the door, returning shortly with a large, battered tin box. He took out a tube of salve and gently applied the ointment to the bites on the dog's back haunch and the gashes across its nose. "If they don't start to heal in a day or two, I'll take her to the vet." Benny rubbed his face next to the dog's ear. "We missed you around here."

"Did she always have a leg missing?" Sharon asked.

"Johnny found her in a hunter's trap. She was just a pup, and the leg had been broken so bad no one could do anything about it. The vet was going to put her to sleep, but Johnny asked the doctor to cut it off and sew her up because he was taking her home with him."

"What'd Julie say to that?"

"They weren't together back then. He always liked dogs. He has a way with them."

"Well, this dog wanted in here real bad last night."

"She used to live here. Julie refused to have the dog in the house when she and Johnny got together, so the best place turned out to be The Nowhere. But after a while, Julie didn't want her in the bar either. Said it made the customers uncomfortable seeing a dog with three legs. She made Johnny keep Three Toes outside in the back yard. And then one day, Three Toes just up and took off. We'd see her from time to time, running with a pack of dogs, but she never came back to the bar."

"I guess she knows this is a safe place," Sharon said.

"Dog's are smarter than people, if you ask me." Benny opened the wood stove. "The fire's almost out. I think we need to keep her warm." He shoved a large hunk of timber onto the embers and then inspected several wounds on the dog's back. "You did a good job of cleaning her up. Looks like you might have done this before."

"Might have," Sharon responded.

"Johnny's going to be real pleased to see this old gal again. He never said much, but I think he got pretty upset when he thought she'd gone wild."

"She made up her mind about what was best for her and took off," Sharon said.

"Suppose so." Benny reached into the brown paper bag that he had set down on the floor beside him. "Here's your coffee. And I brought doughnuts. Three Toes used to have a fierce sweet tooth. I'll bet she'd sure go for some of these right now." He opened the package.

The dog's ears perked up, and she lifted her wounded snout from her folded paws.

"She remembers." Benny put one of the powdered sugar delights in front of her nose. "I used to feed her these things all the time. I could get her to jump in the air and catch one."

Three Toes licked the doughnut.

"Here, girl, take the whole thing."

The dog gobbled it down in two bites.

"I'd love to sit here all day by this warm fire and keep Three Toes company, but I got things to do." Benny patted the dog gently on the top of her head. "I'll see you later. I sure hope Johnny's feeling better today. Maybe seeing his old dog again will perk him up. I wish he'd listen and see a doctor." Benny went behind the bar. "Looks like you'll have enough fire wood for the next day or two." He hoisted up the box of empty beer bottles from behind the counter.

Sharon got up from the floor and stretched. Three Toes licked at a dusting of powdered sugar near her paw. "I should probably cook up a couple of burger patties for her. Looks like she hasn't eaten in a while."

"Good idea, but be careful how many you let Julie know you feed this dog. She's not going to be happy seeing Three Toes again." Benny headed out the back door. "See you later."

The dog lowered her head once again to the floor, and Sharon went into the kitchen. As she cooked some meat, she thought the floor could probably use another good cleaning before the place opened up. Loading a paper plate with the cooked meat, she put it in front of Three Toes, and before she went back into the kitchen to mop the floor, she put the remainder of her quarters into the jukebox.

Sharon slapped the mop across the kitchen floor, keeping time with the tune. Music made her feel good. She opened the back door. The rain had stopped sometime during the night and turned to snow in the early morning hours. A small layer of snow lay on the ground, and the wind had blown a drift against a broken-down tool shed sitting farther out in the woods. Moose tracks marked up the recent snowfall, and it looked like the animal had been munching on a puny birch sapling growing next to the old shed, nearly stripping the scrawny tree of its thin limbs and bark during the night.

Sharon threw the bucket of water out onto the snow, leaving a strange fissure across the white surface, making the ground appear as though the earth had cracked open. She stood in the doorway, the frigid air brushing against her face, and she sang along with the jukebox. At first, her voice came out in a soft whisper, her words a quarter of a second behind the singer. Then she sighed, caught the timing, raised her voice, and sang to the trees, to the icy terrain, to the hoof prints in the snow, performing to the ghost of who she used to be. Time stood still while she serenaded the snowy landscape. Her hands were cold, and she shoved them down into her jean's pockets and kept crooning, blowing out all the bad air from her lungs, from the lousy life she'd made for herself.

Standing in the shifting gray morning light, she watched a strip of sunlight shimmering across the frozen treetops. Yesterday's storm had brought with it some seriously cold temperatures.

Sharon stopped singing, closed the door, and went back inside where she intended to get a bit more sleep before Johnny or Julie showed up. Three Toes lifted one ear as Sharon walked passed the wood stove. The dog did not attempt to lift her head or move a paw.

With the door closed and only one small window, the back room was airless, cramped, and musty. She lay on the rickety camp bed and pulled a blanket over her shoulders. The cracked photo of her daughter was on the wooden crate next to the bed. Sharon looked at the photo, wondering if children forgave their parents. Nothing she did now could change the past, and Sharon wondered if she had the courage to see Tasha.

She turned off the lamp, closed her eyes, and remembered holding the hot little hands of a sick child with a fever, the furry breath of a baby sleeping at her breast, the excited squeal Tasha made when she discovered a new toy under the Christmas tree.

Sharon lived in such a blur back then she marveled that she remembered anything. The thoughts racing around in her head made it impossible to sleep, and she left the bed and went back out into the bar.

Chapter Five

THREE TOES STARTED TO BARK when Johnny walked into the bar. The dog wobbled quickly to stand at Johnny's side.

"Where the hell did you come from?" Johnny grabbed hold of the dog's ears. "You broke my heart, you old two-timer."

Three Toes licked Johnny's hand, whimpering as though she were catching him up with everything she'd been through since they'd last seen each other.

Johnny looked at Sharon. "How'd she get in here?"

"She was scratching at the back door last night after everyone left. Looks like she'd been in a nasty fight. I cleaned her up the best I could. She's been sleeping most of the day."

"I don't know how pleased Julie's going to be to see her, but damn, she sure warms my heart." Johnny carefully stroked the dog's back. "You happy to see me, old girl?"

Sharon went into the kitchen, leaving Johnny and Three Toes to get reacquainted. A short while later, the front door opened and closed several more times, but Sharon paid no attention to who came in. She got a couple orders and was kept busy most of the night. Close to quitting time, with all the orders taken care of and the kitchen cleaned, she sat on a stool at the bar.

From what Benny said about Julie and old Three Toes, Sharon expected there to be a big row. But you'd have thought spring was in the air by the way Johnny got along with his wife. Julie wasn't smiling and she didn't look any happier than usual, but she hadn't ordered the dog out of the bar either. And she hadn't said a cross word to any one. She sat in her usual seat in the corner booth, smoking, drinking, and talking with the women who hung around The Nowhere almost every night.

Dell showed up late and hadn't brought his guitar. Sharon overheard him tell Johnny, "The little woman's on a tear about something. You understand how it is. It's best to leave a woman to cool down without a man in the house." Dell put a couple of bills on the counter, and Johnny passed him a beer.

It wouldn't have taken much to empty out the place this close to quitting time. No one put money in the jukebox, and the two regulars sitting at the bar could have probably been swept out the door with a broom and they wouldn't have thought anything unusual had happened to them. Julie's lady friends had bundled up and gone home, one helping her drunken husband off a barstool, slapping a hat on his head, not bothering to let the guy button up his coat and pushed him out the door.

Johnny stood behind the bar, wiping the dribbles of liquor from the counter when the roar of a motorcycle engine shattered the quiet. The hair on the back of Sharon's neck bristled. The front door burst opened. A man and a woman tromped into the bar. The man took off his cap and goggles.

"It's our last ride of the year," the woman said. "We're celebrating." She took off her helmet and shook her head. Long, black hair cascaded across the shoulders of her leather jacket. "I want shots of bourbon for my man," she said and pointed to the booth near Julie.

Herb grabbed the woman, and standing next to the jukebox, he loaded up the machine with coins. The music started up, and they began to dance.

Johnny set down two shot glasses on the table and filled them to the brim with booze. Then he went back behind the bar.

Soon the couple stopped dancing and snuggled up in the booth.

The woman threw back her shot of whisky. "This isn't enough to warm shit. We're freezing. Hit me again, bartender."

"We're closing up," Johnny said. "That was the last call."

"The hell it is," Herb said, holding up his shot glass. "I'm ready for another one." And then he caught sight of Sharon. "Well, well, if it isn't the fish kicker. I thought this place smelled fishy. Hey," he said to his companion, "I want you to meet this year's fish kicker. Oh, that's a mighty powerful woman sitting on that stool over there. How you been, you old stinky thing?"

"I thought they threw your ass in jail," Sharon said.

"Hey, they can't keep an innocent man locked up. No witness. No evidence. You can't convict a man on thin air." Herb smiled broadly. "I'll bet you're happy to hear the good news. You must have been so worried about me."

The woman roared with laughter and then called to Johnny, "We need another shot over here, Mr. Bartender."

Johnny looked at the clock above the bar. "You get one more drink, and then I'm closing up."

"Pity, and this is such a charming place," the woman drawled.

Johnny took up the whisky bottle and poured them both another shot of booze. "Now mind you," he said, "I don't want to be responsible for you folks getting hurt after drinking too much at my place and then getting into an accident on that icy road out there. Only fools would be riding motorcycles with these road conditions."

"Ah, now isn't that considerate of you." Herb downed his drink and pointed a finger in Sharon's direction. "Mind you, don't let that fish kicker smell up your place or people might stop coming here."

Sharon didn't think Dell had paid much attention to what was going on. He looked a little pie-eyed when he came to the bar earlier, and he hadn't done much talking most of the night. But she thought it must have been the tone in Herb's voice that made Dell arch his back and then jump off the bar stool, beer bottle cradled in his hand as he glared at the biker.

Herb put his shot glass back on the table, clenched his fists. "You want some of this, old man?"

"Don't get any ideas about starting a fight in here," Johnny warned.

Julie seemed disinterested in what was going on. She lit another cigarette and swallowed the last of the whisky in her glass.

Dell climbed back onto his barstool and took a long drink of his beer.

"Thought so." Herb let out a deep-throated, evil chuckle that made chills travel down Sharon's back.

"Benny," said Johnny, "take Three Toes outside for a late night stroll before we lock up the place."

Benny patted the dog on the head. Three Toes followed Benny to the door.

"That is about the ugliest dog I have ever seen," said Herb's companion.

"I guess you guys like freaky things around here," Herb said.

"Finish your drinks," Johnny said. "It's time to go home."

"The night's still young," Herb said.

"Spend it somewhere else. I'm closing up."

"That's not very hospitable," Herb said.

"I don't aim to be at this late hour."

Sharon turned her back to Herb, though she could see him in the mirrored wall next to the cash register, nuzzling his face into the neck of his companion. He brushed her long black hair aside and kissed her neck. She reached up, touched Herb's face. The woman had a large spider tattoo that spread out across the back of her hand. When she first came into the bar, with her hair draped across her face, she had looked like a younger woman. Now with her face exposed, the black hair pulled back, she looked old enough to be Herb's mother. Her hand stroked Herb's face, and it looked as though a spider had crawled up onto his cheek as they sat kissing and whispering to each other.

Johnny folded up his mopping cloth and threw the last beer bottle into the box under the counter as Benny returned with Three Toes.

Julie stood and brought her whisky glass and ashtray to the counter. She stepped to one side of the wood stove and flicked the lights switch off and on several times. "Party's over, folks. Time to take it home."

"How about another round for the road?" Herb asked. "We just got started."

"Go start up someplace else. You heard the man. The bar's closed." She flicked the lights on and off again, tapping her foot impatiently on the floor.

"It's easy to see who wears the pants around here." Herb got up from the booth, and taking hold of his girlfriend's hand, he brought her close to where Sharon sat.

The girlfriend sniffed at Sharon. "I see what you mean. She does smell like fish."

"Told ya," Herb said. Then opening the front door, he called back over his shoulder, "See you around, fish kicker."

"Friends of yours?" Julie raised an eyebrow at Sharon.

"Hardly," Sharon replied.

"What's this fish-kicker thing about?"

Sharon got up from the barstool and headed for the kitchen.

Julie looked angrily at Sharon. "We don't need their kind hanging around our bar. I know Herb. He's been nothing but a pain in the ass for any bar he sits in."

Sharon turned, looked directly at Julie, and said, "You want me out of here, you got it. Fry your own damn burgers. I don't need that jackass biker, and I certainly don't need you down my neck. Just say the word, and I'm gone."

"Now, now," Johnny said. "No one said anything about you leaving. It's late, and we all need some sleep."

Julie glared at him.

Benny put on his hat. "I'm out of here."

Dell threw back the last of his beer. "How about a ride home, Benny?"

"No problem."

"What do you intend to do with that dog?" Julie snapped.

Johnny looked down at Tree Toes. "Don't know yet."

"I thought we'd said good riddance to that thing long ago."

Johnny put on his coat. "I'm going home," he said.

Julie grabbed her coat and walked to the door.

"See you tomorrow," Johnny said.

Three Toes lifted her head and softly whimpered.

The three cars started up outside, the sound of the engines sharp in the cold air. There was the crackle of gravel in the parking lot as they drove away and then silence.

Chapter Six

WHEN EVERYONE WENT HOME AND The Nowhere was empty, Sharon put the small stack of quarters Johnny left for her by the cash register into the jukebox before she went into the kitchen to finish cleaning up. Herb's appearance at the bar tonight spooked her, and she slid the deadbolt across the doorsill of the back door.

After cleaning, she turned out all the lights and, with only the glow from the jukebox, put a couple of logs into the stove before sitting on the floor next to Three Toes. She stroked the top of the dog's head. "How are you doing, old girl?"

Three Toes lifted her muzzle slightly. A broken-hearted tune played on the jukebox. Last night, Sharon had not planned to fall asleep on the floor, but tonight, her actions were deliberate. It made her uneasy to think about bedding down in that cramped back room. She leaned against the wall and sang along with the music.

The jukebox went quiet. She looked down at Three Toes. "You know these songs?"

The dog did not stir. The next tune began, and Sharon sang along, right on time, right on key. She could almost feel the muscles in her throat relaxing as the air passed across her vocal cords, and with each new song, her voice became stronger.

When the quarters ran out and the jukebox went silent, Sharon went into the back room, grabbed a blanket, and curled up on the floor between Three Toes and the stove. She had no problem falling asleep, but when she woke, half caught in a dream, nothing made sense, not sleeping on the floor, the dog, or the nearness of a warm stove.

Sharon thought she heard a child crying. Was it a dream? She sat up and listened. The wood in the stove crackled. Three Toes shifted a back paw and then made a soft yelp. What time was it? How long she had been asleep?

Then the back door rattled. Three Toes lifted her head and growled.

"Easy, girl." Sharon got up and went into the kitchen.

She wanted to ask who was at the door but decided against doing that. Someone pushed hard on the door, and then they turned the doorknob.

"Sharon!" Benny called out.

She pulled back the deadbolt and opened the door. A dull gray light filtered through the trees. Benny stood on the top step, a load of firewood cradled in his arms. A brown paper bag sat on top of the logs.

"Why'd you bolt the door?"

"No reason." Sharon didn't think it was anyone's business how nervous seeing Herb again made her.

"Let me in. This is heavy."

Sharon stepped aside, and Benny hurried into the building.

Three Toes came into the kitchen and gave a few greeting yelps.

Sharon took the paper bag, and Benny quickly walked through the kitchen and dropped his load onto the floor next to the stove. He dusted off his hands and then bent down to take a close look at Three Toes. "She'll be back to normal in no time." He opened the paper bag, took out the coffees, and handed one of the hot cups to Sharon. "So, what's this fish-kicker business?"

"It's nothing."

He took a drink of his coffee. Sharon knew he was dying to know more, though he didn't ask another question. Instead he looked at Three Toes. "Want some breakfast?" he asked and opened the package of doughnuts.

The dog's ears perked up.

Benny tossed her one of the sweets, and the dog gulped it down in one bite. The dog looked at Benny, anticipating another doughnut. "One more," Benny said and tossed Three Toes another doughnut.

Sharon sat back down on the floor, leaned against the wall, and sipped her coffee. The dog wagged her tail, and with only one hind leg to support her rear end, the dog's entire backside wobbled back and forth.

Sharon sighed heavily and looked out into the room. "You think we could take a ride some day?" she asked. In the last year, she had pushed the thought of ever seeing her daughter again back so far it didn't even have a shadow. But some things just wouldn't stay hidden, and she had to at least try to make it right again.

"Sure. Any time you want. I thought maybe you had something against cars you walking all the time."

"I got nothing against cars. I just don't have one."

"You tell me when and where."

"What would you say about doing it today?" Sharon hadn't planned to ask Benny for a ride. The words came tumbling out of her mouth, and she figured it probably had something to do with the strangeness of her dreams leaving behind a mental grease slick of remembrances.

"I got nothing going on."

"You know Cooper Landing?"

"Yeah."

"I'd like to take a ride out that way."

"You want to go now?"

"We could." Sharon looked down at Three Toes. "How about we take her with us?"

"Fine with me. I got my dog in the truck, but the cab's big enough for everyone. I've had more than one party in that rig. What do you want to do in Cooper Landing?"

"I might want to visit someone. Not sure yet." Her pulse beat so quickly it made her light headed.

With some difficulty, Three Toes climbed into the cab of the truck. Benny's dog, a white husky, greeted Three Toes as though they'd been old lost friends. They sniffed each other and yelped excitedly.

"Get in the back, Whiskey. Go on, get!" Benny said sharply, and the husky clambered into the jump seat under the rear window. The two dogs lay muzzle-to-muzzle, and though they still did a bit of yelping, they stayed put.

Sharon scooted into the cab of the truck. It did look like he had plenty of parties in his truck. Candy wrappers and coffee cups were scattered on the floor, and bits of dried dog food crunched underfoot. An empty water bottle was wedged in an open space between the radio and the glove compartment while a stack of unopened junk mail littered the top of the dashboard. The seat was covered in dog hair, and the air smelled strongly of dog breath.

Benny climbed into the driver's seat and started up the engine. "It takes a while for the heater to get going. Hope it's not too cold for you."

"It's fine," Sharon replied.

Once outside in the fresh air, Sharon realized she hadn't left The Nowhere much since she'd taken the job as fry cook. The early morning air was damp and dark, and gray clouds hung low in the sky.

A little way down the road, Benny asked, "You know exactly where you want to go? Or you just want to ride around in Cooper Landing?"

"Don't know yet," she said.

"I can do that," he replied.

A female moose and her adolescent calf stood at the edge of a wooded area, pulling at a mangy bush. The bit of snow that had fallen a couple days ago had melted in the sleet, leaving the earth looking pretty muddy. The mother moose stood in muck up to the middle of her shins while her offspring with its sharp small hooves sunk even lower into the muddy mess. It didn't look like the bush would make it through the winter if the animals kept chewing at its branches. Food could get pretty scarce for the animals in some areas, and once a young tree had been spotted, only a miracle would see it through until the new growth started up again in the spring.

Sharon knew the road very well. They passed the gas station where she'd purchased groceries and freshened up in the bathroom. Then they drove near the section of the road where Sharon used to turn off and travel into the woods where she'd spent the summer nights in the hunter's lean-to overlooking the bluff. It sure didn't look inviting now with the early winter weather and dampness dripping off the branches and the sky heavy with the possibility of even worse weather on its way. Soon Benny drove past the gravel driveway that led to Willie's fish weigh station. She couldn't see what was going on back there, and she wondered if Herb's bike was parked in the yard.

A little farther up the road, Benny broke the silence. "When we get to Kenai, you want to take a look across the inlet and see what's going on with old Redoubt? I haven't felt any quakes in the last few days, but I hear they still think it might blow its top."

"Yeah, sure," Sharon replied. She wasn't in a big hurry to get to Cooper Landing, and maybe she'd even lose her courage and ask Benny to turn around before they got there. It was a long shot, whether she'd have the nerve to knock on her mother's door. Chances were good her mother wouldn't let her into the house even if she did manage to step onto her family's front porch.

Benny turned the truck off the main drag and drove down a small paved road in back of a retirement home. A landslide had caused part of the pavement to slip over the edge of the cliff, and the highway department had built a metal guardrail along the bluff. Benny parked the truck as close to the edge as he could, though there wasn't much to see across the inlet. The clouds covered the mountains all the way down to the shoreline. Chunks of ice had begun to form in the bay, and steam drifted out from where the warm Kenai River met the cold water at the mouth of the bay.

"I'm going to let the dogs out to do their business." Benny opened the door of the cab, and the dogs scrambled onto the road. A roar of cold wind came bursting into the truck. "I thought I'd take a walk, but this wind is for the birds." He climbed back into the driver's seat. "I heard that if you can see a plume of smoke above all these clouds, we're in trouble and that old Redoubt is on her way to blowing her top. I don't see anything, do you?"

"No, it looks like always," replied Sharon.

The dogs came back to the truck, scratching at the door to be let in.

"I guess they're not so crazy about the wind either."

"Probably hurts their ears," Sharon said.

Benny let the dogs in, turned the key in the ignition, and drove back to the main road. "Want to listen to some music?" He turned on the radio.

Soon, a familiar tune came on, and Benny began to sing. It didn't sound like he could carry a tune if his life depended on it. That didn't seem to bother him, and he just kept singing.

Sharon took pity on him and joined the sing-along. He looked over at her and smiled. "You've got a great voice."

She said nothing and sang. The music occupied her mind, and for a short while, she forgot about Cooper Landing and what might be waiting for her there.

They drove for another hour, singing from time to time as they traveled into the foothills. Sharon knew the area like the back of her hand. She'd traveled the road many times, both sober and drunk. They passed the rafting company she'd worked for during the summers while she was in high school, helping to pack the catered lunches and, when she got older, taking people out on the river.

She closed her eyes. Her heart raced. They were not far now from where her mother lived, and Sharon scooted down into her seat, turning her head away from the window, fearful that someone in a passing car might recognize her.

"Are you all right?" Benny asked.

"I'm fine." When they reached the dirt road that led to her mother's house, she said, "Turn here."

Benny made a quick right turn. They traveled a short distance on a badly rutted lane until they came to a Y in the road.

"Left," Sharon said.

Benny veered left.

They went a short distance further, and then Sharon said, "You'll pass a couple of turn-offs, take the third one, and it's going to be on your right."

"Where the hell are you taking us?" Benny said as they hit a couple of nasty dips in the road. The truck wobbled from side to side before Benny made the right hand turn.

"Stop," Sharon said.

She looked up the road at the small white house only slightly visible through a cluster of pine trees and underbrush. Several of the neighborhood children ran in the front yard, and she knew Tasha was probably there with them as they chased each other around the house. Just barely visible in a section near one side of the house that the family used to park cars, she saw her brother's beat-up camper. There would have to be some fence mending with him, too. Of everyone in her family, he had tried the hardest to get her to straighten out.

She rolled down her window. The children's laughter rang out crisp like little bells.

Whiskey whimpered and began to scratch at the truck's door.

"Stop it, Whiskey!" Benny said.

The dog sat on her haunches, but continued to make shrill whining sounds.

"I can't do it," Sharon said under her breath. "I just can't do it."

Benny didn't ask any questions and waited.

They sat for a short while longer. Sharon watched the children run up onto the porch and then go into the house. In their absence, the only sound was the branches of the old trees rubbing across each other as the wind blew through the tops of the forest.

Chapter Seven

SHARON DIDN'T SING ON THE ride back to the bar, though Benny had the radio on. He didn't say much, either. The dogs rustled slightly from time to time but mostly slept. The remaining bit of daylight quickly turned to dusk once they reached the main road, and by the time they arrived back at the bar, the late afternoon sky had turned winter black.

Several cars sat outside The Nowhere when Benny pulled into the parking lot.

"Looks like folks are getting an early start," he said.

Sharon got out of the truck. Three Toes and Whiskey tumbled out behind her and scurried along the trail that led into the underbrush. She went into to the bar while Benny waited for the dogs to finish their business.

"Where you been?" Julie grumbled.

Sharon didn't respond and went into the kitchen.

Several regulars sat in a booth, playing cards and sucking on bottles of beer.

Julie followed her into the kitchen. "Did Benny come back with you?"

"Yeah," she replied.

"I need him to work the bar tonight. Johnny's sick and decided to stay home."

Sharon turned on the grill, took out several stacks of patties from the freezer, and put them into the refrigerator. She washed her hands and slipped on an apron.

Benny opened the door and stepped into the bar.

"Good, you're here," Julie said. "Johnny's sick. You have to work the bar tonight."

"How bad is he?" Benny asked.

"Who knows. He's always got something wrong with him these days. But my arm's still giving me trouble, and I can't lift and hoist all those bottles tonight." Julie rubbed her shoulder and then looked down at Three Toes. "I was hoping that she'd run off again. I'll never know what you see in that dog."

The door opened, and a cold wind raced across the floor. Dell's black cowboy hat was the first thing Sharon saw as he stepped through the doorway. This evening, he not only brought his guitar with him but a small child stood next to his skinny legs. She was a dainty little thing with a tiny nose and an impish face poking out from a big fur hat. She hesitated at the entrance.

"Come on, Rose," Dell said and gently nudged the little girl into the building.

Behind Dell was a waif of a woman with large, dark intense eyes that nearly took up most of her face. The woman wasn't much taller than the child, and she wore an oversized man's coat that made her look even shorter than she probably was.

"I brought my family with me tonight," Dell called out to Julie as he headed for an empty booth.

This was the first time Dell brought his family since Sharon had started working at the Nowhere.

"Great," Julie said. "That's all I need is a family of freeloaders."

"Sings for his supper, doesn't he," Sharon said.

"Barely," Julie responded. "Petunia's no dummy, and I'll bet she's smelled another woman's perfume on old Dell. He talks a big game, but she's got him on a short leash, and she's not going to let him get away with anything. Not like his first and second wives."

"Who's tending bar tonight?" Dell called out.

"The bum hasn't even taken off his coat, and he's looking for a free beer," Julie grumbled. "Benny, go take care of him."

Benny headed for the bar, and Three Toes hobbled off with him.

Julie stood in the doorway of the kitchen for a short while longer, leaning against the wall, rubbing her shoulder. The front door opened again, and several people stepped into the building, bringing with them bursts of freezing air. It didn't take long before The Nowhere was filled up and Sharon was knocking out the hamburgers.

As usual, the kitchen was busy until around ten o'clock. Then the orders tapered off and drinking was the only thing on the minds of people who would hang around until closing time. Dell sang a couple of short sets, and Sharon hummed along with the tunes. The music made the evening go faster and lifted her spirits.

Dell's daughter poked her head into the kitchen once. "Hi. What's your name?"

Sharon greeted the child. The skittish little thing ran back out and scooted beside her mother.

At one point, when the call for burgers had stopped, Sharon stood in the doorway of the kitchen, watching the people interact. The serious drunks did the least talking and sat hunched over their booze. Several women sat in a booth smoking cigarettes, playing poker, and throwing back shots of whiskey.

"Hey, Sharon," Dell called. "I hear you sing pretty good. You want to join me?"

Sharon looked annoyed at Benny.

Dell slipped out from the booth and headed for the corner of the room where he kept his guitar. "Come on. Let's sing a song." He began to pick out the melody to Weeping Willow, the big hit by that female country star who died too young in a plane crash. "Come on. Don't be shy. No one bites you for singing." He began to sing.

Sharon slowly moved toward Dell, feeling like everyone was staring at her as the music pulled her closer to the guitar. A familiar tingle started in the pit of her stomach. She cleared her throat, and then right on key, she joined Dell in perfect harmony. He smiled and let her finish the song solo. The words came easily to her, the tune and the rhythm flowing as though she were in a dream.

When she finished singing, everyone applauded. It was a small audience, and even though most of the people at this hour were quite drunk, they'd stopped what they were doing and listened.

"Okay, fry cook, what else do you know?" Dell asked.

"You start something, and I'll finish it," she replied.

Dell picked out a few notes, and then without an introduction, Sharon began to sing a standard old country tune. Dell gave her a sly look, and though he joined her for a few lines, he let her do most of the singing.

Everyone in the place tapped their toes as Sharon sang, and even the two drunks sitting on barstools by the draft beer pulls looked like they were enjoying the entertainment.

"Let's give it a rest," Dell said. "You always want to leave them aching for more. Benny was right. You sing very well."

"Thanks," Sharon said and sat down on one of the empty barstools. She glared at Benny. "You traitor."

"I thought everyone should know how good you sing," he responded and then flipped open a bottle of beer and took a swallow. "You want one?"

"No."

"Yeah, right, I forgot." Benny took another swallow of his beer.

Sharon couldn't explain, not even to herself, why it felt so good to sing. It just did, and she thought it best not to look too close for a reason.

The women playing cards gathered up their coats and pocket books and left the bar. Soon, the only people left in The Nowhere were Dell, his family, and the two drunks.

Rose had fallen asleep stretched out in the booth next to her mother. Dell looked like he could still go on talking to Benny and drinking beer for a couple more hours, but when Petunia put on her coat and woke up the little girl, Dell got his gear together and put on his coat, too.

As Dell and his family were about to leave, the front door swung opened, and in walked Herb with his dark-haired friend hanging on his arm. They removed their coats, and the woman headed for an empty booth.

Herb stepped up to the bar. "Two tall cold ones," he ordered and looked around the bar. "Quiet night."

Benny put two draft beers on the counter without responding.

"Where's the regular bartender?"

"Don't know," Benny said.

Herb looked at Sharon. "Get your ass in the kitchen, and fix me two burgers."

"Grill's closed," she said.

"You always were lazy and worthless. I suppose you're too stupid to make an exception?"

"Watch your mouth," Benny said.

The biker took up the beers. "It's a free country, ain't it?" He joined his girlfriend at the table. He whispered something in her ear and motioned in Sharon's direction.

A slight smile slid across the woman's face as she glanced over.

Dell took his coat off and sat back down. He leaned over the table and said something to Petunia and handed her a set of keys. His wife gathered up the little girl and hurriedly left the bar.

Julie had been watching from her usual seat. It didn't look like she'd consumed much booze, but the ashtray in front of her overflowed with butts.

Dell got up from the booth and stood next to Benny. "I told Petunia to go home. I said I wanted to stick around for a while."

Benny leaned on the counter.

"I thought you could use some help if things get out of control," Dell said.

"I think they're too dumb to start any trouble," Benny said.

"Never underestimate anyone."

Herb tossed Benny a quarter. "Put some music on. You'd think someone died in here."

"You want music, do it yourself." Benny flung the coin back at him.

"That's no way to treat a customer."

"I don't know you from a hole in the wall, and most regular customers pick out their own music." Benny cleared the counter of a couple empty bottles.

One of the drunks sitting on a barstool stood up, put on his coat, walked to the door. He called back to Julie, "Hope Johnny feels better soon."

Julie nodded but said nothing. Her girlfriends had only stayed at the bar a short while, and most of the night, Julie played a game of solitaire. She looked at her wristwatch. "Benny, let's close up the place," she said and loaded her deck of cards back into the box.

"I'm not done drinking," Herb said. "You did this to me the last time I was here."

Julie slid out of her seat. "Well, we'd love to have you come earlier. Spend some quality time with us."

"I'm not going," Herb said.

"The hell you're not," Julie said.

Benny reached under the bar and eased the barrel of a rifle out from under the counter. He hadn't taken his eyes off Herb or his dark-haired woman friend.

Herb saw the rifle, too. He smiled. "You don't intend using that on me because I want another drink?"

"No," Benny said, "but if I were you, I'd be afraid that it might accidentally go off. You never can tell about these old guns. They don't always work right, you know. And I can't remember the last time Johnny used this thing. The old thing could probably use some cleaning."

Herb stood up, bent over, fixed the pants legs around his boots before he looked up at Julie. "You always clear out your place this way?"

"Just for special customers," she replied.

Herb's upper lip quivered into a sneer. Sharon knew that look. A chill crawled across her shoulders as she remembered the night he came looking for her in the woods.

"It's my place," Julie said. "If you don't like the way I run things, then don't come back." She snubbed out her cigarette. "Everyone, get out of here! Go home."

"All right, don't get your panties twisted," Herb said. He looked at Sharon. "You need a ride, fish kicker? My friend and I would be glad to drop you off."

Sharon turned her back on him.

"Well, is that a nice way to act when there's an offer of kindness?" Herb taunted her.

"Some people just don't know how to be polite." Herb's woman friend brushed a large strand of black hair from her face. It looked like a spider had crawled up onto her head.

"You folks are a bit too jumpy, if you ask me," Herb said.

"Just tired, young man. Now shut up and go home," Julie said and she attempted to shove her good arm into a coat sleeve. The coat slipped out of her hands and fell to the floor. She bent down to pick it up, but every time she leaned forward, she grabbed her arm and winced.

"Want some help?" Sharon asked.

"Suppose I do."

Sharon got down from the barstool and held the coat while Julie continued to struggle with her one good arm. "I hate being so damned helpless." Julie muttered so softly that even Sharon barely heard the words. She picked up her pocketbook from the table. "Benny, close up the place." She walked to the door, held it open, tapped one foot impatiently on the floor, and looked back at Herb. "Okay, you two, it's time to leave. Come on. I don't have all night."

Herb and his girlfriend took their time. Then, just before Herb stepped outside, he stopped. "Fish kicker, you sure you don't need a ride?"

Julie stepped out and slammed the door shut. A chill hung in the air. Benny dropped the empty beer bottles into the bin under the counter.

"Is that guy an old boyfriend of yours?" Dell asked, a curious smile on his face.

"Hardly," Sharon replied.

"He's certainly got his sights on you." He drank the last of the beer in his glass.

Sharon glanced down at the floor.

"You sure don't say much, do you?" Dell said.

"Some folks say I talk too much."

"I think you sing better than you talk." Dell got up from the barstool and stretched. "Benny, how much longer are you going to be closing up?"

"Almost there. Just got to lock up the cash register, and then we're out of here." But after Benny had locked up the money, he picked up the broom and began to sweep behind the bar. He gathered up the bits of dirt in a dustpan. He looked at Sharon. "You going to be all right?"

"I'll be fine." She went into the kitchen.

Benny gathered up his coat and hesitated by the bar. "You sure you're going to be all right?"

"Go home. It's late. And take that cowboy singer with you."

Benny stood in the opened doorway. A fierce wind blew into The Nowhere. He started to say something but apparently changed his mind and closed the door behind him.

Chapter Eight

SHARON LOCKED THE DOOR. IF she'd had a day like this last year, she would have hit the bottle big time. Seeing the children playing in her mother's front yard earlier that afternoon was like seeing a ghost, a haunting of her past. The laughter of the children resonated in her mind like one of the old faded tunes she now sang to herself in the kitchen. After seeing Herb again tonight, the urge to have a drink pulled hard at her. The craving for booze never really stopped. She bit her lip, hoping that tomorrow would be easier.

She stood at the kitchen sink, running cold water over her hands, trying to cool the fever that raged deep inside her bones.

Next time, she told herself, next time she'd meet her mother face to face, convince her she'd changed. Sharon wanted her daughter back, and after a year of sobriety, she'd do whatever it took to make that happen.

Three Toes brushed against Sharon's leg and whined impatiently.

"Benny forgot to take you for a walk, didn't he?"

The dog sat lopsided on the floor, flicking her tail back and forth.

"All right. Let me dry my hands, and I'll let you outside."

The frigid wind blew through the woods. Halloween was only a couple days of away. There had been several days of freezing temperatures and then another snowfall tonight. A thin sheet of frozen snow glistened in the moonlight. The trees cracked and groaned under the weight of the gathering ice.

A stream of light spread out across the snow from the opened doorway. Three Toes hobbled down the stairs and hurried to the area Benny cleared earlier for the dog to use during the winter months.

Sharon sat on the bottom step. She couldn't see much of the northern lights tonight. Most of the strong colors were happening on the far eastern horizon and hidden by the tall branches of the tree.

Three Toes barked.

"What's up, girl?"

The dog growled deeply.

Footsteps crunched on the snow and approached quickly. She stood up and called to the dog. "Come here, girl."

Three Toes continued to bark.

Two figures stepped into the streak of light from the open kitchen door. Herb and his dark-haired woman friend stood there, grinning at Sharon.

"Well, fish kicker," Herb said, "you getting some fresh air?"

"What do you want?"

"I just happened to see a light back here and thought I'd see what was going on."

"Bullshit," Sharon said.

"I'm a curious fellow. You should know that about me by now."

"Come here, Three Toes," Sharon called.

The dog stood her ground and continued to bark.

Herb eased forward.

Sharon moved up one step. "If it's money you want, I've got none."

"I don't want your stinking money, fish kicker."

"Then what do you want?"

"You and I need to have a little talk." He stepped closer.

Scrambling up the steps, Herb grabbed her wrist before she could get into the kitchen. She tried to pull away, slapping at him with her free hand, but Herb got hold of her other wrist.

"I just want to talk with you, fish kicker. Don't get nasty with me."

"What do you want?"

"You and I need to come to an understanding."

"What's that?" Sharon asked.

Herb jerked her down from the stairs. She lost her footing and he flung her to the frozen ground. Sharon lay atop the snow, one elbow bloody from skimming across a shard of broken ice.

Three Toes jumped and barked frantically until Herb's girlfriend slammed her on the head with a flashlight. The dog whimpered and tumbled over onto the ground.

"You, bastards," Sharon cursed.

"Never can tell what a freaky dog like that will do. Now, maybe you and I can have a nice chat without all that yelping," Herb said.

"What do you want, Herb?"

"I have a feeling you think I had something to do with that biker they found in the bay this summer."

"You're crazy," Sharon said. "I didn't see anything, and if I did, that's my business."

Herb slapped Sharon across the face. "You're wrong. It is my business, and I intend to make sure you keep your mouth shut. Or I'll have to close it permanently."

"Threatening me isn't going to keep the law from figuring things out. They already have a pretty good idea you were in on it. What are you going to do, beat them up, too?"

"You're a stupid fish kicker. I know all about your lame family." He kicked her in the thigh. His upper lip quivered. "Get up."

Sharon managed to stand. Her shirtsleeve was torn, and her elbow stung sharply.

Three Toes began to stir and attempted to lift her head.

Herb glared at Sharon. She clenched her fists. "What are you going to do, you stinking old fish kicker, attack me?" Herb asked. "You going to hit me with those fists?" He laughed at Sharon, and just as he opened his mouth to say something else, she let him have it with a right cross to the temple then a quick upper cut to his chin. His eyes rolled back, and he crumpled to the ground.

Herb's girlfriend rushed at her, swinging the flashlight like a club. Before she could make contact, Sharon crashed her fist into the woman's jaw. She fell to the ground, blood dripping from one side of her mouth.

Three Toes, still wobbly, barked furiously, her snout only inches from the woman's bloodied face.

"Come here, girl," Sharon shouted, and though Three Toes continued to make one hell of a racket, the dog trotted to her side. She grabbed Three Toes by the scruff of the neck and dragged the dog up the stairs. When she reached the doorway, she looked back at her would-be attackers. They both looked pretty stupid sitting in the snow, rubbing their chins, trying to figure out what had hit them.

"I'll get you for this," Herb shouted.

"Sure, you will," Sharon mocked. "When spring comes to Alaska in December."

Sharon pulled Three Toes into the kitchen, but before she closed and dead-bolted the door, she gave one parting shot, "I wouldn't sit in the snow too long or your balls will freeze to the ground. If you have a pair, that is."

Chapter Nine

SHARON'S HEART THUDDED LIKE CRAZY against her ribcage, and the veins in her neck pulsed so fast she thought her head would explode. She switched off all the lights in The Nowhere. The darkness comforted her. The outside world went deathly silent, and she wondered what Herb would do next to intimidate her.

It took a few minutes to get her bearings before she went into the bar and sat on the floor next to the stove. She leaned against the wall, waiting, listening. Three Toes lay next to her.

Sharon hadn't slept in the back bedroom since that first night Three Toes showed up, and she had no intentions of shutting herself up in that cramped musty room tonight. Gathering up her blanket, she bedded down between the dog and the woodstove. She lay on the floor and with every sound—the creaking walls, a passing car, the crackling log in the woodstove—she wondered if Herb had hatched a new plan. Three Toes whimpered in her slumber, scratching at the floor in a worrisome dream. Eventually, Sharon fell asleep.

Benny arrived earlier than usual and, accustomed to finding the bolt across the back door, knocked and called out for her to let him in. Three Toes woke first and yelped anxiously until Sharon opened the door and let Benny tromp in with an armload of wood, two cups of coffee, and a package of powdered sugar doughnuts.

"What the hell happened last night?" Benny asked. "There's blood on the snow." Sharon took the bag from his hand. "Had some company."

"You okay?"

"I'm fine."

"Was it Herb?"

"Yep. But he and his lady friend got the worst of it. It wouldn't break my heart if I never saw those two again."

Three Toes jumped up on Benny's leg. He patted her heartily on the back. "You want your treat?" Benny handed the dog a doughnut and then looked at Sharon. "So, what is it between you and this guy that he comes around causing trouble?"

Sharon took one of the coffees and headed out to the bar. She turned on the light above the cash register.

"I don't mean to pry," Benny said. "But do you owe this guy money?"

"I don't owe him shit."

Benny stepped behind the bar and poured a hefty shot of booze into his coffee. Three Toes lay down near the stove.

Sharon leaned on the counter to drink her coffee. She winced at the pain in her forearm and elbow, which she had forgotten about until then. Blood was caked on her shirtsleeve.

Benny put his coffee down on the counter. "I suppose you didn't take care of that last night?"

Sharon shrugged.

"Thought so. I'll get my first aid kit." He hurried out to his pickup truck and quickly returned. "Roll up your sleeve. I'll wash it off with some disinfectant."

Sharon pulled up her sleeve and inspected the long scrape on her forearm. It didn't amount to much, but Benny poured the disinfectant onto a wad of cotton and dabbed at the wound until it was clean. Then he smeared salve over the area and covered it with a band-aid.

"That should do it," he said.

"You're becoming a regular doctor around here," Sharon said.

Benny gathered a few empty beer bottles from behind the counter and tossed them into a cardboard box. "Why does this guy keep coming around?"

"You got too many questions," she replied.

"Maybe I do." Lifting the box from the floor, he placed it on the end of the counter before taking a drink of his coffee. Though he did not look at her, she knew he waited for her to say more.

Three Toes stood up and paced back and forth in the room.

"Suppose she needs to go outside," Benny said as he walked to the front door.

The dog quickly followed and scooted outside into the cold morning air before Benny had a chance to step out onto the gravel parking lot. Sharon stood in the doorway. Benny climbed into the cab of his truck while the dog hurried into the scrubby pine.

A thick freezing mist hung in the air, and Sharon could barely see the gas station across the road. Just then a yellow school bus came into view. The driver honked, waved, and the vehicle continued on its way, vanishing up the road into the morning fog.

Benny climbed back out of his truck and waited for Three Toes to finish her business, and then they both came back into the bar. He handed Sharon a revolver. "I want you to have this."

Sharon did not take it. "What do I need a gun for?"

"Just keep it. You flash this in anyone's face and watch them scramble for the woods."

"I can't take this."

"The hell you can't," Benny said. "You either take it, or I don't leave here."

"You're overreacting."

"I don't think so, and I know Johnny would agree with me. Herb's a nutcase and who knows what he'll do next." Benny placed the gun on the counter next to the draft beer pull handles.

Guns were not foreign to Sharon. She'd been handling them since her father and older brother thought she was strong enough to manage the kickback. They said she was a good shot for a girl, and she'd been on plenty of hunting trips. It wasn't the gun that bothered her. What worried her was the possibility she might have to use it on Herb. Benny was right. Herb was unpredictable, and on top of that, he was stupid. That made for a lethal combination.

Sharon took a drink of her coffee.

Benny sat on the barstool next to Sharon. He fiddled with his pack of cigarettes and drank some of his spiked coffee. "I brought a couple cans of dog food for Three Toes so you wouldn't have to use up the hamburger patties."

Sharon looked down at the dog. "She's a good watchdog."

"That's what Johnny always told Julie, but Julia wouldn't hear a word in the hound's favor. I'm surprised she hasn't kicked the dog outside by now." Benny took a doughnut from the package. Three Toes lifted her head, twitched her ears, and he tossed her the treat. "I have the safety on." He scooted the gun closer to Sharon. "Put this some place where it'll be easy to reach."

Sharon looked at the gun. "I really don't need this."

"Need it or not, I'm leaving it here."

She sighed. Too many things pushed and pulled at her, and she thought she'd probably be better off if she could get just a little drunk. Last year, she'd wintered over so saturated with booze she hardly felt the cold and she worried about nothing in those days. The temptation to have a drink gnawed at her like an angry rat, trying to fight its way out of a cage.

Benny lit a cigarette. He blew the smoke into the cool morning air. "You might want to put more wood on the fire. I hear it's going to get pretty cold today." He tapped a bit of ash into his empty paper coffee cup. "There hasn't been any more news about Redoubt, so I guess we don't have to worry about any volcano erupting."

Sharon took another drink of her coffee.

"I have some errands to run today," Benny said. "And then I'll swing by and see if Johnny's going to show up at the bar tonight. He wants me to do some work in the back room. I guess you'll have me around for a couple of days. Hope you don't mind?"

"Suit yourself," Sharon said.

Benny stood and headed for the front door. "I left the dog food in the kitchen. I shouldn't be long, but if I were you, I'd keep this door locked until someone else was in the bar. And put that gun someplace safe."

Benny closed the door behind him. Sharon locked the door and heard Benny start his engine. The gun sat on the counter, the muzzle pointed toward the cash register. If she had to, she would use it. And that frightened her.

She toyed with the few coins in her pocket. Instead of sticking the money into the jukebox, she went to the pay phone, flipped through the pages of the directory, found the number for the social services office in Kenai, and dropped the coins into the phone. Sharon never stopped thinking about her daughter. Even in her drunken state, the little girl came to her in dreams. And though she realized that her desire to hit the bottle would probably always be there, she wanted to know if, after a year of fighting this demon, she could bring her life back to normal. Before she could lose her nerve, she dialed the number.

The breath caught in her chest when the woman on the other end of the line said, "Hello."

There was a pause. Sharon could not find her voice, nor would her lips form the words.

"Hello," the woman said again.

The person on the other end of the line hung up.

Unable to move, Sharon stood by the phone. Three Toes lay next to the wood stove. Half asleep, the dog sighed heavily. A diesel truck downshifted as it roared past The Nowhere. She knew it wouldn't be easy to contact social services, but she had no idea that it would be this difficult even before she'd begun getting her daughter back.

Sharon looked at the bottles of booze lined up along the mirrored wall. *God, what I wouldn't do for a drink right now.* Pacing back and forth for several minutes, she put a quarter into the jukebox and randomly picked a tune. The music only slightly lifted her spirit. Taking a deep breath, she picked up the receiver again, this time determined to at least say something.

"Hello," the voice on the other end of the line said.

Sharon paused and cleared her throat. "Is Patty Smalls there? Can I speak to her?"

"One minute, please," said the woman.

Sharon had been on Ms. Smalls' caseload for a couple of years, and she didn't know if the woman still worked in the same office, but she had to begin somewhere.

"Yes, this is Patty Smalls. How can I help you?" The voice was familiar, soft and slightly self-conscious.

"Ms. Smalls, it's Sharon. Sharon Wolf."

"Oh, my, how good to hear from you. How are things going?"

Sharon hesitated. A flood of memories came rushing at her, and she remembered Ms. Smalls had tears in her eyes when Tasha was taken away and placed in the custody of the courts. Confused and hung-over, Sharon sat in the Judge's Chamber's more than a year ago with only one thing on her mind—her next drink. Now she could hardly breathe the desire to see her daughter weighed so heavily on her chest.

"I'm doing better," Sharon managed to say.

"That is so good to hear."

Silence. Sharon wondered whose turn it was to talk, and she trembled with anticipation.

"What are you doing these days?" Ms. Smalls asked.

Relieved to have direction, Sharon said, "I'm a fry cook."

"Really? How nice. Around here?"

"Up the North Road," Sharon said.

"Do you have a place to stay?"

"Yes."

"Are you drinking, Sharon?" Ms. Smalls asked.

"No. Not for almost a year."

"I am so glad to hear that. So, why are you calling me today?"

"I want to see Tasha," Sharon said. These words come so much easier than she thought they would. The fear that she'd never be allowed to see her daughter again had kept her from forming such a sentence until now.

"You know your mother has custody of Tasha?"

"Yes, I know."

"I'll call her and see what I can arrange," Ms. Smalls said. "I am so glad that you called. Where can I reach you?"

Sharon looked around the room, panicked. There was no way she'd leave the telephone number of The Nowhere. "I don't have a phone. I'll have to call you in a couple of days."

"That'll be fine," Ms. Smalls said. "I hope…." She paused. "I'll do everything that I can, Sharon. Goodbye."

Sharon hung up the phone, her ears ringing from the tension. It seemed as though the conversation had gone on for hours, yet it had only been a minute or two. Her body went limp. She had done it. She had taken the first step.

Three Toes stood up, yawned, and stretched.

"I'll bet you could use something to eat." Sharon walked into the kitchen. Her hands still trembled when she reached into the drawer, scrambling through the utensils looking for the can opener. If making the phone call to Ms. Smalls had been this hard, how difficult would the next steps be? As she emptied the canned dog food into a dish, she realized how much her drinking had cost her and worried she'd never have the opportunity to prove to her mother that things had changed, that she had changed.

Chapter Ten

SHARON HAD JUST FINISHED STRAIGHTENING out the kitchen and settled down with a soda when Benny banged on the back door.

"A storm's blowing in from the north," he said when she opened the door. "It's going to be a big one."

Before Benny could step into the kitchen, Whiskey bounded in through the doorway. The dog scrambled into the middle of the room and shook its body until nearly everything within reach had been splattered with wet globs of snow.

Three Toes hobbled into the kitchen.

"Julie called this morning," Benny informed her. "Johnny had a bad stomach attack in the middle of the night, and she took him to Kenai Emergency. They admitted him." Benny reached down and rubbed Three Toes' snout. "I went to see him. Looks like they're going to keep him for another day or two."

"What do they think is wrong with him?"

"Don't know. But he looks bad. I mean he looked green."

"So, what now?"

"Julie said she'd come by this evening, though when I saw her at the hospital it didn't look like she'd gotten much sleep herself. I told her I'd manage The Nowhere. She wouldn't agree to that. If you ask me, I think everyone's going to have to sit tight until this storm passes." Benny took off his coat. "A while back, I promised Johnny I'd hang some sheetrock in the back room. Looks like this is a good time to get started."

When Sharon took the job as a fry cook she hadn't planned on getting caught up in other people's business. Now she was trying to undo her own messed up past while sitting in the middle of a stranger's bad luck. She threw the bolt across the back door, went into the bar, and shoved another log into the woodstove.

"Where did you put the gun?" he asked.

Sharon sighed. She wanted to tell him to either take the gun back or she was going to shove the thing down his throat, but she knew he wouldn't take it back. "I stuck it behind the gallon jar of relish on the shelf by the back door in the kitchen."

"That's as good a place as any."

The back room certainly needed some fixing up, and Sharon didn't know if Johnny had really wanted all this work to be done now or if Benny had decided to hang around, wanting to see if Herb would show up again.

Benny spent a good part of the day nailing sheetrock to a couple of crumbling walls and plastering over the seams. Sharon offered to help, but he said he preferred to work alone. So, she sat in a booth playing solitaire, drinking sodas and listening to the wind wailing away outside. The dogs got feisty late in the afternoon, and she took them outside to jump around in the new fallen snow. They made a royal mess with their snow-caked paws when they came back inside, and she mopped up the place again while the hounds settled down for a nap next to the stove.

When Benny finished in the back room, he poured himself a double shot of booze, made a hamburger, and put a few coins into the jukebox. "You know, it's Halloween. We might have some party-goers tonight. Probably even a few of them might be showing up in costume." He settled himself into a booth, lifted his legs up onto the seat, closed his eyes, and took a nap.

By evening, the snowfall was so heavy the plows couldn't keep the roads clear. Julie called before the first customers showed up, and Benny came into the kitchen to give Sharon the good news.

"Julie's not coming in tonight. She said the battery in her truck went dead. I asked if she wanted me to come by with jumper cables or give her a lift to see Johnny at the hospital, but she said her uncle was coming by in the morning with a new battery. And as far as Johnny was concerned, she said he could manage his health problems without her meddling."

It took Benny the better part of an hour to clear the parking lot as best he could with the plow hooked to the front of his pickup. Anyone who came out in this weather had a snowplow attached to the front of their vehicle and were expected to plow part of the road as they headed back home again later that night.

Even with the storm blowing outside, a few of the regulars showed up at the bar. One woman, a drinking buddy of Julie's, came dressed in a frilly white dress with a strange lacy cap on her head. She stomped the ice and snow off her boots, making a noisy entrance as she headed for the bar.

"Guess who I am tonight?" she asked one of the regulars sitting on a barstool.

He gave her the once-over and shrugged his shoulders.

"Bo Peep," she said.

"Well, I guess you do look like a sheep herder." He took a swig of his beer and then said, "Hey, Benny, give Peeps a beer."

Because this was the first big snow storm, and Halloween night, the handful of people who showed up were in a festive mood. Someone brought a box of drugstore chocolates and left it sitting next to the draft beer pulls. One of the regulars, a woman who did as much dancing as she did drinking, brought a plastic container of Squaw Candy, an Alaskan salty treat of smoked strips of salmon.

Dell didn't show up so someone was always dropping coins into the jukebox. Benny asked Sharon to dance when she stepped out of the kitchen to drink a soda. She shook her head.

"No, I don't know how."

He looked disappointed and went back to polishing glasses behind the bar. "You should learn. If I can do it, anyone can figure it out."

The bar was lively most of the night, but the storm made everyone uneasy and even the heaviest drinkers eased up on the booze earlier than usual. The Nowhere emptied out a little after midnight. Sharon made short order of cleaning the kitchen. After slapping a mop across the floor to dry up the puddles, she was more than ready to get some sleep and laid out her blankets next to the stove.

"Me and Whisky are going to stay the night," Benny said. "I'll bed down in the back room. It'll give me a chance to see if I nailed the wall in good enough." He grinned. "If you hear a crashing sound back there, come pull me out from under the mess."

"I'm sure you did a good job," Sharon said. "You know you don't have to stay on my account."

Benny looked away. "I'm not driving in this weather."

Sharon crawled under her covers. Benny flicked off the lights, and the only sound in the room came from the wind howling and banging against the doors. In the early morning hours, the snow turned to freezing rain, and a thunderous cracking sound beat against the outside walls of the building. It sounded as though a tree had fallen against one side of the building.

Three Toes roused first. Barking furiously, the dog could not be consoled. Then in the back room, Whiskey started up.

Benny ambled out into the bar and turned on a light. "Three Toes, you're a pain in the ass," he grumbled and then sat in one of the booths for a while looking blankly at the floor.

Whiskey stopped howling but continued to whine and whimper.

"I'm making coffee," Benny finally said. "Want some?"

"Might as well." Sharon slowly got up and followed Benny into the kitchen. She hadn't looked forward to seeing so much of Benny when he'd insisted on hanging around after the incident with Herb. She'd figured that his constant yammering would drive her nuts, but he surprised her and they'd actually done very little conversing. And though he hadn't said a word about it, she knew he was curious about that trip up to Cooper Landing and then that scuffle she'd had with Herb and his girlfriend.

After making the coffee, Benny opened a couple cans of dog food, dumping the contents onto two separate paper plates. Three Toes ignored the food and scratched at the back door to be let out. Benny unlatched the bolt, and the dog scooted down the stairs and into the freezing morning. Whiskey came into the room, sniffed at the food, and then headed outside to join the other dog.

Sharon knew that once she started to try to get visitation with Tasha, Ms. Smalls was bound to make inquiries. That was her job, and her snooping around would certainly open a can of worms. Everyone around The Nowhere was bound to find out about her drinking, the trouble with keeping jobs, and the difficult relationship she had with Tasha's father. They'd learn everything about her that was none of their business. As much as she hated thinking it was bound to happen, she knew there was no other way if she wanted to eventually get Tasha back.

Benny handed Sharon a cup of fresh brewed coffee.

"I'll make us breakfast." She beat half-a-dozen eggs in a bowl and poured them onto the hot grill. While they cooked, she threw several handfuls of potatoes into the bubbling grease, and in no time, breakfast was prepared. Sharon and Benny brought their plates of food to one of the booths and sat facing each other. Sharon could tell from the sweet smell of bourbon on Benny's breath that he had spiked his coffee, again.

"Always drink your breakfast coffee with a kick?" she asked.

"Sometimes," he replied, stabbing at the eggs with a fork. "You don't drink much, do you?"

Sharon looked down at her plate of food. "Used to."

Benny lifted a forkful of eggs but stopped before he stuck them into his mouth. "I tried that once."

"Tried what?"

"Tried to stop. I'm not too good at that kind of thing."

"I guess you have to want to stop." She took a big swallow of her coffee.

"Suppose so," he said.

After eating, Sharon needed fresh air, and she opened the front door. A major part of the storm had passed during the night, and the small bits of sleet that continued to fall tinkled on the frozen crust of snow. A soft, hazy light glowed along the eastern horizon. It still wouldn't be daylight for hours.

Across the road, a ribbon of steam floated up from the exhaust of a pickup truck parked in front of the gas pump at Phil's place. A plow had come by earlier and done its best to clear the road, but a thin sheet of ice glistened on the pavement under the lights of the mini market's sign.

"I think I'll go over and visit with Phil for a while," Benny said. "Want to come along?"

"Sure," Sharon replied. "We take the dogs?"

"Phil's not going to let them both into his place, but they'll occupy themselves."

A lone pickup truck slowly eased along the snow-packed road as Sharon and Benny trudged across the parking lot. A half-foot of snow had fallen during the night, and the top layer, a thin crust of frozen sleet, rang out like a breaking pane of glass with each step. They waited at the road's edge for the pickup to pass. The dim morning light gave the vehicle a soft dreamy quality, and when it passed, Herb snarled at her from the passenger seat. He rolled down the window and glared at her as the pickup continued on its way and then disappeared up the road.

"You ever going to tell me what's going on between you and that guy?" Benny asked.

"It's nothing." She stepped out onto the road. The pavement, slick with ice, made the crossing treacherous. Even the dogs had difficulty crossing to the other side, but Phil had scattered shovels of sand in the open space around his gas pumps, making the walkway near the store less slippery.

Benny opened the door to the shop. As he stomped the snow from his boots, he told Phil and a customer sitting in one of the chrome kitchen chairs near the wood stove about Johnny's hospitalization.

A teenage girl sat on a stack of firewood near the stove, stroking a husky sitting at her feet. Sharon had only seen the girl once before, but mostly she'd seen the girl from a distance pumping gas at the station. Now looking at her close up, Sharon could see by the eyes and cut of the jaw that she was Phil and Beverly's daughter.

Beverly sat on a stool behind the counter. "That's a shame about Johnny," she said.

"Hope it's a short stay," Phil said. "Can't abide those places myself."

"You ask me, Johnny's got an ulcer," said the guy sitting on one of the kitchen chairs near the wood-burning stove.

"And I know who gave him the ulcer," Benny said. "He would have been better off setting up housekeeping with a she-bear than hooking up with Julie. At least that way, the bear would have slept through the winter, giving Johnny some peace and quiet for a while."

"That's enough, Benny," Phil said. "It's Johnny's choice. No one asked your advice."

"You're right, Phil," said the guy sitting near the fire. "It's none of our business. But Johnny was a perfectly healthy man before he got mixed up with that woman. I've known him since he was a kid, and he was never sick a day in his life."

"Could be he's just picked up a flu," Phil said.

"Flu my foot," Benny said. "That woman's going to be the death of Johnny."

Ignoring Benny's last comment, Beverly asked, "So, Sharon how are you doing over there?"

"I got no complaints."

"Why don't you tell them about Herb's visit with you the other night and you knocking him and his girlfriend on their asses?" Benny said.

Sharon glared at Benny. "You're a regular newspaper today. It's no one's business."

"When was this?" Phil asked.

"A couple days ago," Benny chimed in.

"Why didn't you come over and tell us?" asked Beverly. "What brought this on?"

"It was nothing. I took care of things myself."

"I want you to promise me," Phil said sternly, "if Herb or anyone comes around again and starts trouble, you get your butt over here as fast as you can."

"I can manage myself." Sharon poured herself a cup of coffee and took a chocolate bar from the candy counter. She reached into her pocket and took out a couple of dollar bills.

"Your money's no good here," Phil said. "Coffee and sweets are on the house this time of the morning."

"How about the cigarettes?" Benny asked.

"We should charge you double," Beverly said.

Benny winked at Sharon and sat down on a pile of logs next to the teenage girl. "How you doing, Linda? Are you still working for that dog breeder?"

"Yep," Linda said. "We got a new litter of Husky pups the other day, and we're gearing up for the Iditarod, so I got lots to do."

Benny reached down and stroked the dog.

"I see Three Toes is back," Linda said.

"Hope she doesn't run off again," Benny said.

"It's like old times watching her running around." Beverly poured herself a cup of coffee. "Did Linda tell you she's going to race in the Junior Iditarod?"

"That's great," Benny said. "I thought about doing that when I was younger, but it just never happened."

"It takes a lot of work to get a dog team ready for the race," Phil said. Sharon saw the pride on Phil's face, and though he didn't seem to be the kind of guy who did much smiling and bragging, his face lit-up as he talked about his daughter. "Linda's been out every day and some nights, too, getting her dog team ready."

Sharon watched the dogs running back and forth in front of the store. Three Toes always in pursuit of Whiskey but never far behind and both dogs seemed to have reconciled themselves to the start of the colder weather.

A few customers hustled into the self-serve gas station, and forgoing small talk, they handed Beverly their money and then hurried back out into the cold.

"I don't care what time of the year it is," Phil said, "folks are always in a rush to get to work this early in the day. We got a doctor up the road, lives on the other side of the lake, and he's always in a hurry. You'd think the world was on fire the way he rushes out of here some mornings."

The sun, trying to shine through the clouds, turned the sky an ugly grey. The dogs sat at the front of the store. Whiskey scratched at the door to be let in.

"Guess it's time we head back across the street," Benny said.

"You need anything, Sharon?" Phil asked.

"No, I'm fine. Still have plenty from what you brought the last time. Thanks for the coffee."

"And I mean what I said, if anyone causes you trouble and you're alone, get your ass over here."

"Will do," she said.

"Before you go, Phil and I were talking the other night," Beverly said. "It can't be too comfortable living and working at the bar."

"It's okay."

"We thought we'd offer you to stay in our son's trailer. It's parked in back of the garage." Beverly sighed heavily. "Looks like he's not going to be around for maybe a year. His regiment is being sent to the lower forty-eight before they're deployed to Afghanistan." Beverly's eyes filled with tears, and her voice cracked. She glanced at her husband and then quickly looked away.

Phil cleared his throat. "It's winterized. It's small but fully furnished, and we'd let you stay there rent free. Think about it. You'd be doing us a favor. The winter is rough on empty trailers, and Charlie would appreciate someone looking after it in the rough weather. It's a real cozy little place."

"Thanks," Sharon said. "I'll think about it."

Beverly turned her back to the door. She took the filter from the coffee maker. Her shoulders trembled softly, and Sharon suspected that she was crying.

Benny opened the door. The dogs barked excitedly. A strong wind blew into the mini mart, and the howling winter weather rushed into the warm little room.

"Thanks again for the offer," Sharon said and hurried out into the cold. She got half way across the parking lot when she glanced up the road. The same pickup truck they saw earlier sat in a newly plowed area on the shoulder of the road. Herb glared out the passenger side of the windshield, looking back at Sharon.

Benny saw the pickup, too. "Don't expect I'll be going any place today," he said as they stood on the porch to The Nowhere, stomping snow off their boots before going into the bar.

The dogs followed Sharon into the kitchen and gobbled down the food Benny set out for them earlier that morning. Sharon took a small stack of patties and a couple bags of buns out of the freezer.

"Why don't you tell me about Herb?"

"I don't have to tell you anything." Sharon slammed the freezer door shut.

"Suit yourself, but whether you tell me or not, I'm not leaving you alone as long as he's hanging around out there." Benny went behind the bar and poured himself a tall shot of whiskey. "I got all my creature comforts right here. Why should I leave?" He crawled into one of the booths, put his feet up on the seat, and took a swallow of his drink.

Sharon pulled out a couple of quarters from her pocket, slipped the coins into the pay phone, and dialed Patty Smalls' number. With each ring of the phone, her heart raced faster.

"Child and Family Services," a woman with a dry voice said.

"May I please speak with Ms. Smalls?"

"Just one moment." The line clicked, and then awful music began to play.

It felt like an endless wait, and Sharon could see Benny from the corner of her eye glancing at her from time to time. She wasn't in any hurry to tell Benny her story. She'd certainly messed things up, and now she had to make it right. He'd find out about her life soon enough.

"Hello, this is Ms. Smalls, how can I help you?"

"Hi, it's Sharon Wolf. Were you able to contact my mother?"

"Yes, Sharon, I called your mother right after we talked. She has some concerns, but she's willing to talk with you. I suppose you know it won't be so easy. We still have a long way to go with this."

Sharon's heart beat frantically, and her words caught in her throat. "I understand," she managed to say.

"Would you be able to come to my office tomorrow afternoon

around one o'clock?"

"Yes," Sharon said.

"Good." Mrs. Smalls paused before adding. "I don't know if your mother will bring Tasha."

"I am ready to do whatever I have to. I want my daughter back with me," Sharon said.

"That's the spirit. I'll see you tomorrow. Goodbye."

The line went dead, and Sharon hung the receiver back on the hook.

"I'm going to need a ride tomorrow," she said to Benny.

"Back to Cooper Landing?" he asked.

"No, just into Kenai. I have some business to take care of."

"Sure. Maybe I'll stop by and see how Johnny's doing."

Chapter Eleven

BENNY DIDN'T SAY MUCH FOR the rest of the afternoon and didn't ask why Sharon needed to go into Kenai. She thought his curiosity had gotten the best of him when he asked where in Kenai she wanted to go. But before either of them could say another word, Julie showed up.

"I've only been away one day," Julie said as she stormed into the kitchen. "And look at this place. It's those dogs." A deep scowl creased the space between her eyes. "Those animals have dragged every bit of crap from outside into the bar. Letting that lame dog stay in here was enough trouble, but now I see you've set up a kennel in my absence."

Sharon said nothing, realizing she had to mind her tongue or she'd get fired. Julie was on a tear, and everyone was fair game. Sharon had worked hard to make sure that the place didn't look any different than it always did. It was clear Julie just needed to complain.

"The health department would close us down in a heartbeat if they walked into this place right now." Julie sighed heavily. "I can't do everything myself, and the last thing I need now is for health inspectors breathing down my neck with Johnny in the hospital."

"It won't take me long to mop the floors and get everything in shape." Sharon went into the closet to get the bucket and a mop. She put enough disinfectant into the water for Julie to get a good whiff.

"See that the kitchen is up to standard, too," Julie called to Sharon and then looked at Benny. "Make me a drink. The roads are a mess, and driving here was horrible. And another thing, I thought you were responsible for clearing the snow from the parking lot. I could hardly get into the place. I don't know. I suppose you think you can get away with shirking on the job when Johnny's not here."

Benny poured a double shot of Bourbon into a tall glass, filled it to the top with water. Julie settled into her usual booth and pulled a large manila envelope from her pocketbook. Benny placed the drink on the table.

"Watch what you're doing," Julie grumbled. "You almost spilled on my papers." She sighed and shook her head.

"You hear how Johnny's doing?" Benny asked.

"No. He said he'd call here later this afternoon if they found anything. It's just like him to get sick as the weather is turning cold and I need him around the house to make sure everything's working."

Sharon mopped the dance floor while she listened to Julie complain.

"Did Dell come by last night?" Julie asked.

"No. Only a few of the regulars showed up."

Sharon held her breath. She expected any minute to hear Benny tell Julie about the trouble she had the other night with Herb.

"I want you to give me a count of the bottles stored in the back room," Julie said. "I don't want to run short, and if I need to order, I want to know before it's too late. Between you and Dell getting free drinks, the supply will be gone before winter is over. By the way, how much does Sharon drink when I'm not here?" Julie looked up at Benny, her lips pursed.

"She's a teetotaler. Doesn't touch the stuff," Benny said.

Sharon finished with the dance floor and began mopping around the woodstove. The dogs disturbed by the wet floor got up and went into the kitchen.

"I know her kind," Julie said, ignoring the fact that Sharon could hear her. "It's only a matter of time before she hits the bottle again. Johnny made a big mistake when he hired her. We're a business not a rehab."

Julie complained the entire night, needling Sharon and Benny about the least imperfection. Even the customers weren't off limits to Julie's haranguing. Most of the guys sat with their backs turned to Julie while they guzzled their beers. The woman set the mood for the evening because several women who regularly played cards with Julie sounded more impatient than usual with their men and ordered drinks from Benny with sharp, demanding tones.

When the place cleared out around midnight, one woman smacked her husband in the back of the head when he said he wasn't ready to leave. "You either leave with me now," she said, "Or walk home." And then she gave him another smack with her handbag.

He reached around, grabbed his wife's arm, got up from the barstool, snatched his coat, and stomped out the door.

Finally when the place emptied, Sharon breathed a sigh of relief. She couldn't wait for Julie to leave, but the woman continued to sit in her corner perch, drinking another tall glass of whiskey and water.

Benny appeared in the kitchen doorway. "Sharon, Julie wants to speak to us."

Sharon nodded, and then she and Benny stood in front of Julie like school children, anticipating the worst.

"Benny, get the money out of the cash register. I need to clear up a few things."

Benny quickly did as he was told and returned with the money.

Julie licked her thumb and counted the bills. When she'd finished, she looked up. "Sharon, I have no idea what Johnny said he'd pay you, but from what I see, you're worth no more than the minimum wage. We give you a free place to stay, and that's a triple bonus especially this time of the year. I figure The Nowhere is open an average of seven hours a night, so this should take care of what you've earned so far." Julie handed Sharon a small portion of the money.

Sharon did not bother to count the money. "Thanks. I appreciate this."

"I'm sure you do," Julie said. "And now, Benny, as far as I'm concerned, you do half of what is expected of you. I don't know why Johnny keeps you around. Any way, here's your pay for the week. I certainly hope that while Johnny's laid up, you're more of a help than you've been so far. I need a man around here, not a shirker."

Benny shoved the bills into his pocket.

"I'd like to know what you intend to do with these dogs," Julie grumbled. "We can't have both of them romping around in here, stinking up the place and making a mess of things."

"I still have that work to do in the back rooms," Benny said. "It turns out there's a lot more to do than Johnny thought. When I come here for the full day and then work the bar at night, I can't leave the dog on its own for that long."

"I hope this is not going to be a permanent arrangement."

"I'll work something out," Benny said.

"Make sure you do." Julie sighed, gathered up her handbag, and scooted out of her seat. "It has been such a trying day." She slipped on her coat, leaving the bar without another word.

Benny took a bottle from the shelf and poured himself a tall shot of whiskey. "I can only take so much of that woman." He swallowed the booze down in a couple gulps.

Sharon arranged her blankets on the floor beside the wood stove. She said nothing and lay down, her chest heavy with anxiety. She'd see her mother tomorrow and had no interest in listening to Benny's complaints about Julie.

Benny put his empty glass into the sink and turned off the lights. "Should I put more wood into the stove?"

"It's fine," Sharon said.

Benny stood by the bar, his body silhouetted in the faint moonlight. "You okay, Sharon?"

"Goodnight, Benny. Go to sleep." Sharon rolled over and pulled the blanket over her shoulder.

Benny stood in the dark for a little longer and then walked down the hall, Whiskey tagging along behind.

Sharon could not sleep and lay in the dark, remembering one miserable mistake after another, her past ramming against her mind like wooden splinters hammered into her flesh.

Three Toes shifted a front paw and whimpered softly. The timber on one wall pinged and snapped as the panels shifted in the cooling night temperature. The hard floor pushed against her bones, and no matter what position she lay in, she knew there would be no comfort in sleep tonight. As the full moon slowly crept across the Alaskan sky, a scant sliver of light glowed through the dirty windows on the far side of the bar.

There were so many worries, regrets, and mistakes racing around in Sharon's head that she could hardly distinguish one from the other, and then she heard a dog bark nearby in the woods. Three Toes lifted her head, growling deeply in her throat.

"It's okay," Sharon whispered and petted the dog gently.

The night went quiet, and Three Toes lowered her head.

The moonlight made everything in the bar appear soft and fuzzy. The room grew colder. Sharon shivered, but she realized when she awoke and smelled coffee brewing, that she had, after all, found a little mercy in the long night.

"Morning," Benny said as Sharon stepped into the kitchen.

"Coffee smells good."

"I thought we'd have fried egg sandwiches for breakfast. You could probably use some nourishment before your meeting." The light in the room was dim. Benny sat atop the counter with his dog sprawled out across the floor beneath his feet. "You go fix yourself up. I'll make the food."

Sharon poured herself a cup of coffee and left the room, hoping Benny wouldn't make too big of a mess in her kitchen. She pawed through the bag of clothing Beverly had given her, looking for something appropriate to wear, and settled on a fresh pair of jeans and a flannel shirt. Washing her hair helped alleviate some of the ton of anxious pressure in her chest. Being clean always made her feel better.

Benny surprised her with his ability to fry eggs without breaking the yolks. They ate in silence. He scooped up the last bit of egg that fell from the bun, dumped his paper plate into the trash, and then hurried the dogs outside to do their business. A short time later, he returned and stopped in the doorway to avoid stepping onto the kitchen floor with his muddy boots. "You ready?"

Sharon took a deep breath. For a brief moment, she wanted to bolt, run into the woods, and get as far away from her troubles as her legs could carry her. She stood perfectly still for a moment, then slipped on her coat, and stepped out into the parking lot. It was nearly noon, and sunlight glowed on the top of the trees across the road.

Benny turned the heater up to high, and a blast of hot air hit Sharon in the face as she climbed into the cab of the pickup. The dogs settled in comfortably on the jump seat and did not seem to be bothered by the loud rock and roll that blared from the speakers near where they were scrunched together.

"Want some gum?" Benny asked.

"No, thanks."

Those were the only words spoken until they sat at the traffic light in the middle of Kenai. Benny asked, "You going to tell me where I'm dropping you off?"

"Social Service Agency," Sharon replied. "Make the next left. You'll see the signs."

Benny pulled into the driveway of the agency, and Sharon saw her mother's blue Dodge parked near the entrance to the building. Her heart raced so fast she thought she'd pass out.

"You all right?" Benny asked. "You look pale."

Sharon didn't respond. She couldn't.

Benny looked away and stopped the pickup next to the front door. "I'm going to visit Johnny in the hospital. I'll see what's going on with him. I should be back in an hour. If you're not done by then, I'll wait for you.

Sharon opened the door and stepped onto the icy walkway. The dogs shifted.

Three Toes stood up, and Sharon closed the door before the dog could get out of the truck. Benny rolled down his window.

"I don't know if I can go through with this," Sharon said.

She surprised herself when the words left her lips. Until now, she'd confided in no one, but the fear of not getting her daughter back was too much of a burden to carry alone.

"Do you have a choice?" he asked.

"No, guess I don't."

"You'll be fine."

"I've made a real mess of things," she said and then turned and went into the building.

Sharon remembered the waiting room as a place that favored children with toys and small chairs. In the year before she'd lost custody of Tasha, this had been a place she'd seen at least twice a month. Ms. Smalls had tried everything in her power to make things work out, but back then, it had been easier for Sharon to keep drinking.

Sharon stepped through the door, and her knees nearly buckled at the sight of her mother sitting in a seat facing the entranceway.

"Hello, Mom," Sharon said.

Her mother looked angry. "You got cleaned up."

"Yes."

"Your hair's growing out," her mother said. "You look healthy."

Sharon could see her mother evaluating her, searching for signs of the drunken daughter. She remembered that awful week before the State workers came to take Tasha away, and she knew the old woman had reasons to have her doubts. She'd been drunk for days when her mother pushed through the door and grabbed up Tasha. That time felt like a nightmare. She didn't remember much else about what happened back then, but she remembered being told about the haircut and how it horrified her when she learned that she'd hacked off her and Tasha's hair with a hunting knife.

"Yes, my hair is growing out," Sharon said. A chill ran down her back, knowing that she'd never be free of some memories. She wanted to talk about something else, wanted to ask her mother about her daughter. Had she brought Tasha to the social service office? But Sharon could not bring herself to speak the little girl's name, and she sat in a chair opposite her mother with what felt like a ton of words stuck in her throat.

Chapter Twelve

AFTER THE STIFF GREETING, SHARON'S mother clammed up and sat with a familiar rigidity, her beat-up leather pocketbook sitting on the floor by her feet, her arms folded across her ample chest. The angry glint in her eyes frightened Sharon.

"You look good, Sharon," Ms. Smalls said as she stepped into the waiting room. "How have you been?"

"Fine. I've been fine," Sharon replied.

"That's good. Let's talk in my office." Ms. Smalls turned and headed down a short corridor. Sharon watched her mother follow the social worker and wondered if it was possible to learn to forget. She had been in this building many times, and the place hadn't changed since her last visit more than a year ago. Even Ms. Smalls' office looked the same, with the comfortable easy chairs for her clients to sit in, making the room appear more like a living room in a house than a State office.

"How long has it been, Sharon?" Ms. Smalls asked.

"Seems like a long time," Sharon replied.

"Yes, it does. What have you been doing?"

"Working," Sharon replied.

"Work?" Sharon's mother said angrily. "What do you call work?"

"Please, Mrs. Goodman." Ms. Smalls leaned back in her chair. "Tell me, Sharon, what kind of work have you been doing?"

"I haven't had a drop to drink in over a year," Sharon said.

"I'm glad to hear that. So, what kind of work have you been doing?" Ms. Smalls repeated.

"This summer, I worked in a fish weigh station, and now I'm a fry cook."

Sharon's mother shifted in her chair. "A neighbor told me she saw you sleeping in back of a dumpster."

"That was a long time ago. Things are different now," Sharon said.

Mrs. Goodman leaned forward. "You've broken my heart with your lies and promises. Your brothers and I did everything we could to help you, but you made your own mess, quitting high school then running off and marrying that deadbeat drifter. You thought you knew it all, hanging out with that bunch of losers he called friends. I took you in when he left you high and dry with a kid. And what did you do? Now you have to deal with it." The anger in her mother's face deepened, and the knuckles on her hands turned white as she gripped the handles of the pocketbook she scooped up from beside her feet.

"I don't drink any more, not a drop, and I have a place to stay," Sharon said. She felt a desperate panic that this meeting would not go well.

"I was a fool," her mother said. "I gave you too many chances. Well, it's not up to me any more."

Sharon looked at Ms. Smalls. "I will do anything to get Tasha back."

"It's going to take some time," Ms. Smalls said, "If we work together, you most likely will get custody of your daughter again. But it all depends on you. Do you understand that, Sharon?"

Sharon sighed heavily, and she felt the energy and fight drain from her body. "Yes, I understand."

Ms. Smalls handed Sharon a form. "I need you to fill this out. It's just to let us know what you've been doing since our last meeting. List places of employment and residences. I suppose you know that I will follow up and visit anyone that you put on this list. We have strict guidelines in cases like these where there were charges of possible endangerment and child neglect."

Sharon cringed at these words. Writing down the information about working at Willie's weigh station would be easy, but to explain that she had lived in the woods during the summer might not go over so good. She had no other choice, and she hoped that giving her present residence would be proof of the desire to improve. Putting Julie's name down as a reference might also be a bit tricky, but again, what choice did she have? Sharon felt her mother glaring at her, felt her anger, her disappointment, and her mistrust.

Ms. Smalls shuffled a few items on her desk. "So, Mrs. Goodman, how has Tasha been? I haven't seen her for a couple of months."

"She's been fine, no colds, no flu, and she's doing well in the first grade.

Sharon listened to this conversation while she filled out the form, and though it took her only a short while to complete the paperwork, it felt like it had taken her an eternity. She handed the form back to Ms. Smalls.

Ms. Smalls glanced over what Sharon had written, and then she looked up. "Would you like to see Tasha?"

"She's here?"

"Yes, she's in the play room."

Sharon was nearly paralyzed with fear, and she quickly glanced at her mother.

"Don't screw this up, Sharon," her mother warned. "If you do, you're not going to get another chance. I'll see to that."

Ms. Smalls led them to the back of the building where a room was set up for children to play while their parents met with social workers or attended parenting classes. The top half of the door had been con-structed with a two-way mirror for observation. Sharon stood back from the door. Her heart pounded, her breath caught in her chest, and as she approached the door, her legs felt wobbly and weak.

"Did she know that I'd be coming today?" Sharon asked.

"I told her that you might be here," her mother said.

Sharon looked into the room where one child, a girl with black shoulder-length hair, sat at a table playing with blocks. Tears welled up in Sharon's eyes, distorting her vision.

"Can I talk with her?" Sharon asked.

Ms. Smalls stepped back from the door. "It's up to your mother."

"Mom?" Sharon said.

"I will not let you hurt that child again," her mother warned. She sounded tired but not angry.

"I've made such a mess of things, I know," Sharon said. "I'm trying,

Mom, I really am. I don't want to hurt anyone."

"It's not about you anymore, and it hasn't been for a long time. You do right by that child or you'll lose her for good."

Sharon took hold of the doorknob and turned it ever so slowly.

Tasha shifted in her seat until she sat facing the door. "I knew you would come."

"You did? Well, you were right."

"I'm a big girl now." Smiling broadly, the little girl stood and stretched herself upward. "See how tall I got."

"Yes, you got very tall. And you are still so pretty."

"I can comb my own hair now, too." Tasha ran her fingers through the silky dark tresses.

Sharon sat down on one of the little chairs and wondered if her daughter remembered the hair-cutting incident. "What were you building?"

"Just some old thing."

"Looks like a house or a castle," Sharon said.

"Maybe." Tasha stacked a few more blocks onto her construction. "I remember you."

Sharon stopped breathing for a moment. "You do?"

"Yes, I do. You took a lot of naps, and you were always crying."

"Was I?"

"Grandma said you might not ever come back, but I knew you'd come back for me."

"I missed you," Sharon whispered.

"Me, too." The little girl moved closer to her mother.

Sharon put another block on the structure.

"Did you worry about me?" Tasha asked.

"I worried a lot about you, but I knew that Grandma would take very good care of you."

"Are you going to come and live with us?"

"I have my own place to live," Sharon said. "Maybe you can visit me some day soon. Would you like that?"

"Yes." Tasha put her arm around Sharon's neck and leaned her head against hers.

"I take care of a dog. She only has three legs." Sharon encircled Tasha with both arms and pulled the child close to her breast.

Tasha pulled back slightly and looked at Sharon skeptically. "How can it stand up?"

"Oh, she's a very smart dog. She has a funny walk but stands up just fine."

"Does she fall down a lot?"

"No, I never saw her fall down, not once."

"Never heard of that before," Tasha said.

Sharon gave Tasha a kiss on the cheek.

"I'd like to see that dog," the little girl said.

The door opened, and Ms. Smalls stepped into the room. Sharon's mother stood in the doorway.

"Grandma, did you know that Mom has a dog with only three legs?" Tasha said. Sharon smiled as the little girl's dark eyes danced with excitement.

"No, I didn't know that." Mrs. Goodman glanced at Sharon.

"Can I see the dog?"

"Maybe some day," Mrs. Goodman said. "It's time for us to go home now, Tasha. Remember what I said? We'd visit for a little while, and then I'd take you out for ice cream, and then we'd go home."

"I remember," Tasha said. "But I want to see the three-legged dog."

"Now you have to go with your grandmother and get some ice cream," Ms. Smalls said.

Tasha let go of Sharon and pulled away. "Can I see you again?"

"I hope so," Sharon replied.

Tasha wrinkled her brow and looked at her grandmother. "I don't want to go."

"We have to leave now," Mrs. Goodman urged her granddaughter. Sharon recognized the tone in her mother's voice.

"No!" Tasha swiped angrily at the block structure, and everything tumbled down onto the tabletop.

"Pick those up," Sharon's mother said with exasperation.

"Let's all pick them up," Ms. Smalls intervened. She got down on her hands and knees and began gathering up the blocks that had fallen under the table. "That way, the other children who come here can find them in the box."

Sharon picked up a handful of blocks and dumped them into the toy box. Her mother did not get down on the floor but stood above everyone. Holding her handbag cradled in one arm, she used her free hand to pick up several blocks from the table and deposit them in the box. Tasha picked up a few blocks, and soon everything was in order.

Tasha stood by the door, her face twisted with her effort not to cry. Ms. Smalls had a bit of a struggle to stand up again, but once she'd gotten back onto her feet, she reached a hand out to Tasha.

"I think this was a very good day, don't you, Tasha?"

The little girl stood as still as a statue.

"Would you like to come back here again and play with the blocks?"

"No," Tasha mumbled. "I'm a big girl. I'm too old for blocks. I want to see the three-legged dog."

"Maybe some day soon you will see that dog," Ms. Smalls said. "But now it's time for you to leave with your grandmother and get that ice cream."

Tasha sighed heavily and then hurried down the hall away from the women.

Ms. Smalls extended her hand to Sharon's mother, "Thank you for coming, Mrs. Goodman, and for bringing Tasha. You are doing a fine job with her."

"I just don't want that child hurt again," Sharon's mother said, looking at her. "I won't stand for it."

She wanted to tell her mother that everything would be different from this point on, but the words would not leave her mouth and then her mother turned and quickly followed after Tasha.

"How was that for you, Sharon?" Ms. Smalls asked.

"It was hard. But I meant what I said. I'll do whatever it takes to make this thing work. I'll do whatever you tell me to."

"I'll talk to those people on the list you gave me. We cannot even begin to make a decision before I do some inquiring. If everything turns out okay, then with your mother's approval, we can begin to set up regular visitation for you and Tasha."

Sharon ran her hands through her hair and hooked a few stray strands behind her ears. "What do you think will happen?"

"That's up to you."

"I know."

When Sharon stepped outside of the Social Services Office, the sunshine glared so brilliantly off the frozen snow it hurt her eyes. The sky had become as blue as it ever got, and the thin coating of ice in the trees sparkled as though they had been decked out in diamonds.

Chapter Thirteen

"BEEN WAITING LONG?" SHARON ASKED as she climbed into Benny's truck.

"No." He started the engine. "Johnny's getting discharged from the hospital."

"How's he doing?"

"Seems fine to me. He said he couldn't stand another day in that place. He had some paperwork to fill out before they discharged him. I told him I'd swing by to get him after I pick you up."

Benny turned sharply out of the parking lot. The back wheel ran up onto a mound of ice at the edge of the exit, and the pickup thudded back down onto the icy street. Three Toes yelped, and Whiskey joined in.

"Shut up you two," he shouted, and the dogs settled back down.

A few minutes later, he pulled in front of the main entrance to Kenai Hospital. Sharon spotted Johnny leaning against the wall next to the front door of the lobby, his parka pulled close around his neck. He looked as pale as a ghost.

Johnny opened the door to the pickup. Sharon scooted over to make room for him.

"Let's get out of here before they think of another god-awful thing to do to me," he said and slammed the door shut. "Promise me, Benny, that you won't let Julie drag my ass down here again. I thought they were going to kill me. I'd rather be sick than be taken care of by these devils."

Benny laughed and quickly drove out to the main drag. "You're safe with us."

"Feeling better?" Sharon asked.

"Yeah, I was feeling better before Julie insisted on taking me to the hospital. I don't know what got into her. I told her to let me sleep it off and wait until the morning, but she wouldn't listen and insisted I see a doctor. Hearing her talk to the medical folks, you'd have thought I was on my last legs, the way she was carrying on about how sick I was. I think the poor girl's going to be disappointed that I pulled through."

"They find anything?" Benny asked.

"Not a damned thing. They rammed a rod up my back end and down my throat and damned near drained me of all my blood. All they found was nothing." Johnny reached over the back of the seat and gave Three Toes a hearty pat on the head. "How you doing, girl? You miss me?"

The dog barked a couple of times and licked Johnny's hand.

"So, Sharon, anything happen while I was gone?" Johnny asked.

Before she could respond, Benny blurted out, "Herb came by and tried to strong-arm her, but she knocked him on his ass. We haven't heard from him since."

"What's his problem, Sharon? Why's he got it in for you?" Johnny asked.

"It's nothing."

"Sounds like it's something to me."

"I don't want to talk about it. I can take care of myself," she snapped.

"Okay, okay."

Snow had begun to fall again, and even after the coating of sand that the county work crew spread across the road earlier that day, the pavement was still slick with a thin sheet of ice.

"Damned, it feels good to be out in the fresh air." Johnny stretched out his legs and put his hands behind his head. The color came back into his face.

"You want me to drop you off at your place?" Benny asked.

"No. Take me to The Nowhere. I'll give Julie a call and tell her to meet me there later."

Johnny flipped open his cell phone and hit redial. Looking out of the side window, he waited. Then, after a short while, Sharon heard a small replica of Julie's voice. "Leave a message after the beep."

"Guess she's out," Johnny said.

"Maybe she went into Kenai to see you," Benny said.

"I doubt that."

The day's light turned dusky by the time Benny pulled the pickup into the parking lot of the bar. Several regulars, already parked in their usual spots, were chatting with one another, waiting for the bar to open. A light dusting of snow covered the back of one old guy's shoulder as he leaned into the window of his drinking buddy's car. He looked up and waved to Johnny when Benny turned off his engine.

Johnny waved back. "That guy damn near pays the gas bill for this place." He got out of the truck. "How you doing, Stewart?"

Stewart hurried up the steps, close behind Johnny, nearly stumbling face first into the bar even before Johnny turned on the lights. "It seemed mighty dry without you, Johnny," Stewart said.

"Didn't Benny take care of you?"

"It's just not the same without you," Stewart said as he climbed onto one of the barstools in front of the draft beer pulls.

"I appreciate that," Johnny said.

Stewart leaned his elbows on the counter. "You feeling better? Julie said you were terribly sick."

"Near normal."

"I guess that's a good thing." Stewart locked his legs around the bottom rung of his perch.

"Yeah." Johnny emptied a bag of ice into the bin below the counter.

Sharon went into the kitchen, and set a packet of burger patties from the freezer on the cutting board. She'd been so preoccupied with seeing Tasha that she'd forgotten to prepare the kitchen for the evening before she took off with Benny. There was no telling how many folks would show up tonight, but there were enough patties in the refrigerator to take care of the hungry crowd that might come stomping in out of the cold.

Benny stuck his head into the kitchen. "I could sure use a burger. I haven't eaten since breakfast."

"Sure." Sharon turned on the grill and adjusted the temperature of the fryer. "Want a double today?"

"That would be good."

Sharon tossed a couple of patties onto the hot grill. The meat sizzled and spit. "I appreciate the ride today." The day had gone as good as she could have expected. The visit with her daughter had been far too short, though she felt hopeful.

"Don't mention it." Benny turned and went back out to sit on a bar stool next to Stewart.

Sharon turned the patties and threw a couple of handfuls of potatoes into the fryer. The grease bubbled up and then subsided as the moisture cooked out of the frozen potatoes. She lifted the basket of fries from the hot grease and let them drain while she prepared Benny's burger. She put the burger on a paper plate, dumped the fries alongside it, stuck an extra pickle on the plate, and carried the meal out to Benny.

Sharon perched on a stool at the far side of the counter. Her mind kept playing and replaying the visit with Tasha as though it were a movie. The child's eyes were still wonderfully bright, and Sharon realized how her own selfishness had robbed her of her child's love. She could not forget her mother's critical eyes.

Johnny pushed the damp cloth across the Formica counter top with gusto, looking as jolly as a man with a new lease on life. A few more patrons came into The Nowhere just as the wall phone next to the cash register rang. Johnny lifted the receiver and listened. "It's for you, Sharon." He stretched the cord across the bar to hand her the phone.

Sharon knew who was on the other end of the line. Ms. Smalls.

She took the phone. Her first thought was trouble. Fearing the worst, she hesitated and then put the receiver to her ear. "Hello."

"Well, Sharon your mother just called," said Ms. Smalls.

Sharon held her breath, frozen with trepidation. The music playing on the jukebox faded as did the chatter of the three guys sitting on the barstools next to her. Johnny glanced in her direction and then looked away.

"She's agreed to consider giving you visiting privileges. She's going to make her final decision after I check out your references and do a home visit."

Sharon still couldn't speak. "Did you hear me?"

"Yes. Yes, I heard you," Sharon said, her breath caught in her chest. "What happens next?" She exhaled a lung-full of air.

"Before we can do anything, I'll need to see where you live, where you work, talk to your employer. It's just a formality. I'd like to get this underway quickly. How is tomorrow?"

Sharon's heart raced. "Yes, tomorrow would be fine."

"Good, I'll be there mid-afternoon. I have a few home visits out that way so I'll swing by your place sometime after two in the afternoon."

"I'll be here," she promised. Sharon hung up the phone. There was no way Ms. Smalls would approve of her living quarters. And she was working in a bar. Who the hell was she kidding? She was still an unfit mother.

"What's the matter?" Benny asked. "Looks like you got bad news."

"Yeah, it's bad news." Sharon went into the kitchen.

Chapter Fourteen

IT WAS A SLOW NIGHT. Sharon sat at the bar.

Johnny climbed onto a stool next to her and shuffled a deck of cards. "I hear Phil and Beverly offered you Charlie's trailer."

Sharon looked down at the counter, her eyes diverted away from him.

"Take it." The sternness in his voice startled Sharon. "What do I have to do? Evict you? That trailer will give you a legit residence." He tapped the deck of cards against the counter and shuffled then again. "The Social Services would never let your little girl stay with you if you're sleeping on the floor next to a wood-burning stove."

She watched the deck of cards. "I know. You're right."

"Then, why the resistance when there's only one choice? Let people help you, Sharon. Don't screw this one up." Johnny didn't look at her, keeping his attention on the cards. "We all need help from time to time. No shame in that."

Sharon owned so few possessions it took her no time that next morning to carry them across the icy road and put them in the trailer before Ms. Smalls showed up. It all seemed too good to be true. Clean sheets on the bed, the refrigerator and pantry stocked with necessities, courtesy of Beverly.

"It'll take a while before I can repay you," Sharon said as Beverly came into the trailer with an armload of extra blankets.

"No need for that," Beverly said. "You're helping us out by taking care of this place."

The weather could not have been any worse than it was at the hour Ms. Smalls was to make the home visit. The trailer shook slightly as gusts of wind pushed against the outside walls. Once in a while, a glop of snow fell from a tree limb and thudded on the roof.

Beverly was ensconced on one of the overstuffed chairs, sipping a cup of tea, when Ms. Smalls knocked on the door. Sharon, making last minute adjustments in the bedroom, rushed out to the living room. She knew that Ms. Smalls had gone to The Nowhere first to talk with Johnny. He had promised to be there early to meet with the social worker and then to give her directions to the trailer in back of Phil's gas station.

"She's here." Sharon placed a hand on her chest to try and still her racing heart.

Beverly put her cup down on the end table. "It'll be fine. Just stay calm."

Sharon opened the door.

Ms. Smalls stepped into the living room. "It's really blowing up out here," she said and looked around the room. "What a nice place. Warm, too."

"Would you like a cup of tea?" Sharon asked.

"Would love one." Ms. Smalls brushed the snow from her shoulders. "I'm afraid I've tracked up your clean floor."

"Don't worry. I'll take care of it," she assured her and introduced Beverly to the social worker, making it clear that Beverly and her husband were now her landlords. Sharon grabbed a mop and cleaned the area.

"If you don't mind," Ms. Smalls said. "I have a check list that I must deal with."

"Do what you have to," Sharon said. "I'll make your tea."

Ms. Smalls took a clipboard from her briefcase and began to take notes. "Where is the bedroom?"

Sharon pointed to the back of the trailer. "And the bathroom is on the right." She looked at Beverly's smiling face, and at that moment, Sharon wanted to believe that everything would be all right.

A great crash of wind slammed against the back of the trailer. Mrs. Smalls stepped into the kitchen. "Mind if I look in your refrigerator? It's just a formality. I apologize. We do have to be snoops."

"I understand." Sharon placed a hot cup of tea on the coffee table in front of the sofa.

"This will be a lovely place for Tasha to visit with you," Ms. Smalls said, "though I have to check out a few more things, work references from the summer, and a bit more about your recent history. It will take a little longer than you would like. We have to be sure about how we arrange this visitation. But from everything that I've seen so far, I'm quite hopeful." Ms. Smalls took a sip of her tea. "Mmm, delicious."

It didn't take Sharon long to feel comfortable in her new home, and within the week, Ms. Smalls called Sharon with the good news that everything had been approved and Tasha would be allowed to visit on weekends.

Sharon hired Linda to babysit Tasha on Saturday nights when the bar closed late. That was Beverly's idea. Linda had her days taken up with preparing for the Iditarod, but her evenings were free and it all seemed to be working out perfectly. With the bitterly cold weather, the snow and ice piled higher every day. With Thanksgiving only a week away, everyone came into the bar as hungry as a bear, making cleanup time in the kitchen take longer. Now, Sharon lived for the weekends.

Though Johnny seemed to have an outwardly jolly attitude, he didn't look any healthier than when he'd been discharged from the hospital a month ago. Still, he made it clear to anyone who listened that he had no intentions of seeing a doctor, ever again.

Everyone knew Johnny's tirades were directed at Julie, but she paid him no mind and continued drinking her booze and playing cards with her friends, though these ladies looked up nervously from their hands. Most evenings slipped by in the same manner, the anger smoldering between Julie and Johnny, few words spoken, spiteful looks thrown across the room.

Benny rarely came into the kitchen since Tasha began spending weekends with Sharon. He sat on a barstool and said little. He continued to help Johnny around the place with the odd jobs, and Sharon thought he'd cut back on the number of beers he drank.

One Saturday night, near midnight, the kitchen was clean, and

Sharon dried her hands for the last time that night. The Nowhere was still filled with drinkers. It didn't look like anyone was hungry or in any hurry to leave.

"Doesn't look like the kitchen will get anymore business tonight," she told Johnny. "Okay to leave?"

"Go ahead," Johnny said.

Julie didn't say anything. She didn't even look up, and Sharon suspected she wasn't too happy about having Tasha around on the weekends. As far as Sharon could tell, Julie hadn't spoken a word to the little girl.

When Sharon left the bar, Benny followed her out the door. "It's time I got home, too," he said. "I promised to plow a driveway early tomorrow morning. Some old folks been snowed in for a couple days. One of them has a doctor's appointment, and they need to get their car on the road."

The northern lights undulated slowly across the sky. Colors flashed overhead as a green flame of light ignited a strip of clouds. Benny had cleared the parking lot earlier that day, and a huge mound of ice and snow stood on either side of the building.

He got into his truck and started the engine.

Sharon crossed the street, walked on a newly shoveled pathway that trailed around the back of the mini mart, and ended at her new home. An amber light glowed from a lamp in the trailer's front window. She opened the door, and Three Toes greeted her with a soft yelp. Linda sat on the couch, a book on her lap.

"Everything okay?" Sharon asked.

"No problems," Linda replied.

Sharon removed a few bills from her pants pocket and handed them to Linda, but the young girl would not take the money.

"Maybe next time." Linda put on her coat.

The trailer had a slight musty odor, but it was warm and safe. Sharon went into the bedroom, Three Toes limping along behind her. It hadn't surprised her how well Tasha and Three Toes got along from the beginning. On their first meeting, Tasha, with such a serious look on her face, introduced herself to the dog.

"Hi," she said. "My name is Tasha, and I know you are Three Toes." Then she looked at the dogs missing hind leg. "You walk very good for a dog with only three legs. I'm going to be your friend."

Tasha lay crossways in the double bed. Sharon scooted the little girl's legs out of the way and crawled in the bed. Tasha sighed heavily, rolled over onto her side, and continued to breathe softly.

Sharon loved having her daughter back with her, even if it was only on weekends. She pulled the covers over her shoulders, and it didn't take long before she fell asleep.

Then in a very dark moment, when sleep is welcomed and the dreams have not yet begun, Three Toes barked furiously in Sharon's ear. At first, she thought it was dream. She opened her eyes, and a bright sunlight shone through the window on one side of the trailer. Three Toes continued to bark, and Sharon realized flames were crawling up one side of the wall.

She grabbed Tasha and ran out of the trailer. Three Toes followed close behind, barking furiously. Once outside, a huge flame leapt up into the air while another flame whipped around from the back of the trailer and snapped at them angrily.

The fire lit up the night. A strong odor of gasoline hung in the air. Sharon looked at the gas pumps, wondering if they had caused the fire.

A siren sounded. Tasha, still in a groggy state, screamed and held tightly on to her mother as they moved back from the flames. Phil, Beverly, and Linda ran up the path. Soon, a crowd of people came scrambling out of the bar and rushed toward the fire. They began shoveling loads of snow onto the flames. Several men guarded the gas station, making sure floating sparks didn't ignite the pumps. Presently, a couple of sheriff cruisers arrived, and the officers immediately began to shovel snow onto the fire and tried valiantly to beat out the flames with the shoves.

By the time Benny arrived, the smell of gasoline was everywhere. The flames jumped high into the air engulfing the trailer. He ran frantically around the inferno. "Sharon! Sharon! Where is she?"

"She's safe," Phil said, "but this trailer's done for."

As the snow and ice melted in the upper branches of the nearby trees, a steady rain fell down onto the fire fighters. By the time the volunteer fire department got there, everyone realized nothing more could be done. The crowd backed off from the fire, watching the trailer burn to a shell.

"You and Tasha okay?" Benny asked Sharon.

"We're fine. Scared the shit out of me though. Three Toes is the hero. Her barking woke us up in time to get out." "Where's Tasha?" Benny asked.

"Beverly and Linda took her to their house."

Sheriff Allen stepped out of the crowd and stood next to Sharon. "You got lousy luck," he said.

"Seems that way," Sharon responded.

"I hear you got your kid back with you."

Sharon nodded. It didn't surprise her that the sheriff already knew her business. News traveled fast in this country.

Several men beat on a nearby bush that had caught fire. A wide muddy path now encircled the trailer. The frozen ground was slick with the melting snow.

Phil came from behind the trailer. "Allen, I want you to take a look at something."

Phil led the sheriff, Benny, and Sharon into the underbrush that ran along the back of the property. A bright glow emanated from the burned-out windows of the trailer, and from time to time, they heard a loud popping sound as something inside the trailer exploded. The flames died down somewhat, but the area was still as bright as a summer day, making it easy to walk through the low branches in the surrounding woods.

Phil scanned the darker section of the woods with his flashlight, and then reaching down, he picked up a handful of discolored snow. "Smell this."

"Gas," the sheriff responded.

Sharon smelled gas fumes as soon as she'd opened her eyes, but she thought it was part of her dream.

"See this." Phil pointed a sharp beam of light into the woods. Footprints badly scuffed up the snow and disappeared into the woods. "Well, let's check it out," Sheriff Allan said.

They trudged through the snow and soon found a discarded gas can. After following the tracks for several more minutes, they came to an area where the footprints stopped and snowmobile tracks began.

"This is serious shit," the sheriff said. They quickly walked back to the burning trailer, and Sheriff Allen headed for his car.

"I have a dammed good idea who did this," Benny said.

He started to say more when Phil interrupted him, "Not now, Benny. Let the law take care of this."

News of the fire quickly spread over the icy tundra, and the next night, the bar was packed. So many people were ordering food that Sharon was kept hopping all night between frying up chicken pieces in the pressure cooker and flipping burgers on the grill. And she sure as hell felt like a freak in the sideshow with everyone coming in to take a look at her.

Phil and Beverly offered to let her and Tasha stay with them for the rest of the weekend, and they were willing to keep the invitation open ended until Sharon could figure out what she'd do next. At least she had a place to stay for a while.

"Thanks," Sharon said, and then she sighed. "I don't know if the Social Services will let me have Tasha now that I'm homeless again."

Sharon called Ms. Smalls Sunday morning and left a message about what had happened. When the weekend visitation was over and the social worker on duty arrived to pick up Tasha, Phil and Beverly were there to greet her.

"We have extra bedrooms, and Sharon will be staying with us until she finds new accommodation," Phil told the social worker. "I'll call Ms. Smalls this week and make arrangements for Tasha to stay with her mom at our place during the visitations." He turned to Sharon. "It'll work out. Don't worry."

"I truly want to believe you are right," Sharon said.

Chapter Fifteen

IN THE NEXT WEEK, THE temperature stabilized at twenty degrees below freezing, though that didn't discourage anyone from coming out for a good time at The Nowhere. Dell came into the bar, followed by Petunia and Rose. Petunia tromped the frozen snow from her work boots. The hemline of her long skirt, coated with little chunks of ice, dragged across the floor. The family slid into an empty booth.

"I figured there'd be a crowd tonight." Dell started to unsnap the latches on his guitar case.

"Yeah, it's a curious bunch tonight. We got some folks coming in that I haven't seen in years," Johnny said. "Can't say they're particularly thirsty, but they're sure as hell hungry. Suppose they're wondering what kind of cook Sharon is."

Sharon came out of the kitchen, carrying an armload of burgers and fries. "Hey, Dell. You came to see me perform at the grill, too."

"I'm not your regular ambulance chaser," Dell replied. "Petunia and I thought we'd come by early to see how you were doing. Maybe let Rose play for a while with Tasha."

"She could probably use time with someone her own age," Sharon said. "Right now, she's hunkered down in the kitchen, taking care of Three Toes."

Phil and Beverly had offered to watch Tasha while Sharon worked, but Sharon had a slight panic attack every time the little girl got out of her sight.

When Rose heard Tasha was in the kitchen, she dropped her coat on her mother's lap and hurried into the other room.

"You'd think those girls were sisters the way they became such fast friends so quickly," Del said.

Sharon sighed and looked down at the load of food in her arms. "Well, as you can see, I'm also waiting tables tonight. The orders were getting all mixed up earlier and taking it out to the tables seemed to be the best way to keep things straight. Damn, the way some folks are acting you'd think these burgers were made of gold. A fight nearly broke about whose fries were coming out first."

"Maybe you'd like to do a little singing tonight," Dell said as he hooked the shoulder strap to the neck of his guitar. He strummed the strings, adjusting the tuning.

"That would sure break up the night for me," Sharon said. "But the orders are coming in faster than I can handle them and who knows if another curious crowd is going to come staggering into this place later on."

Sharon went to the end of the bar, unloaded the plates of food, and then returned to the kitchen. She worried that it might be just a matter of time before Ms. Smalls and her mother canceled the visits. Phil and Beverly could not let her go on living with them forever. It seemed like such a long time ago when she'd walked away from her old life, her daughter, her mother, and everyone else who tried to help her. Now, it broke her heart to think that it might all be taken away from her again.

Entering the kitchen, Sharon heard Tasha explaining to Three Toes and Rose, "Tea parties are special times. Even rabbits and foxes go to parties in the forest."

"They do?" Sharon said.

"Yes," Tasha said. "Grandma read that in a book. They drink snow tea in the North Pole."

"I suppose they would," Sharon said.

Rose looked up at Sharon. "Tasha was telling me stories."

Sharon turned her back to the little girls. It was all she could do to keep from crying, and she wondered if her luck was running out. "Would you like some fries?"

"Yes," Rose said emphatically, and Sharon recognized Dell's attitude in that one word.

"Coming right up, ladies," Sharon said.

Tasha and Rose giggled.

"Three Toes is a hero, isn't she, Momma?" Tasha asked.

"Yes. She is a hero," Sharon agreed and dropped a basket of frozen potatoes into the hot oil. The fryer became a cauldron of roaring bubbles.

"Can we have a picnic?" Tasha asked.

"Sure. Just don't make a mess."

The girls arranged three paper plates on the floor. The fries were nearly done. No more orders had recently been called into the kitchen, and Sharon thought that she'd probably fed some of the most curious folks on the Kenai Peninsula. After shaking off the excess oil from the fry basket, she dumped the potatoes into a bowl and set it on the floor between the two girls. Three Toes made a pathetic whimper but didn't try to get at the fries

"Oh, God," Julie groaned, "if the health department ever walked in here tonight, they'd close us down in a heart beat." She stood in the doorway, her hands on her hips. "This is not going to work. That girl cannot stay here."

The two women looked at each other. An uneasy silence hung in the air. Even the girls' picnic chatter had stopped. Julie had not been to the bar in almost a week. No one knew where she had been, and no one complained about her absence, least of all, Johnny.

"And that mangy old mutt is still hanging around here." Julie glared at Three Toes.

"She's a hero," Tasha said.

"She's a freak," Julie said.

Tasha opened her mouth to say something else but reconsidered her words and instead reached over and stroked Three Toes on the snout.

Julie glared at Sharon, walked across the dance floor, and joined her friends at the booth.

The lull in the cooking allowed Sharon time to straighten the kitchen. She had no idea how much longer Johnny and Julie would keep her on as a cook. The trouble with Herb, and now having Tasha around, might just force her to move on. And though she didn't know where she'd go, Sharon wasn't going to let anyone say she'd left a mess behind. For all she knew, Julie could tell her to hit the road tonight after the place closed.

Dell stuck his head into the kitchen. "Sharon, stop that cleaning. We got some requests for live music."

"I changed my mind. I don't feel much like singing tonight, Dell."

"It'll do you good. You know it will."

Sharon looked down at the little girls as they nibbled on the fries and drank their sodas. Three Toes had fallen asleep. For a brief moment, Sharon could have forgotten about the fire, about having her daughter taken away again, and about all the mistakes that she had made.

"It'll make you feel better," Dell said. "Trust me."

She sighed and followed Dell out into the area where he had set up his guitar with a bottle of beer next to the leg of his chair. He picked up his guitar and strummed a few notes of a song Sharon recognized. The room went silent. Sharon felt everyone watching her. She looked down at her feet and waited for the right note and then began to sing. It was an easy first note, nearly effortless. The words flowed. There was no hesitation or loss of power in her voice.

Tasha and Rose poked their heads out of the kitchen door several times, listening to the music, giggling and smiling. Tasha waved to her mother and then scooted back into the kitchen.

Sharon sang several more songs. When Dell hit his stride, Sharon easily followed him as if they'd been performing together for years.

Dell took a couple of swigs from his beer bottle. The bar once again got noisy with talking and the tinkling of glasses. He put the guitar in its case. "That's enough for now."

Sharon climbed onto a bar stool next to Benny, and Johnny handed her a soda. "Thanks."

"No, thank you." Johnny leaned in close and whispered, "It's good to hear something besides Dell's old broken down voice. Refreshing. You know what I mean? But don't tell him I said that."

Sharon smiled. "Mums the word," she said and knew she'd never find the right words to tell Johnny how good she felt at that moment. Slowly sipping her soda, she listened to the chatter in the bar. Someone put coins in the jukebox, and a hard driving rock-and-roll song blared from the speakers. A young couple danced to the raucous beat.

Rose had crawled into her parent's booth and now slept next to her mother. Sharon wondered what Tasha and Three Toes were up to.

"Hey, Johnny," someone yelled. "What'd you do, turn off the heat? It's cold in here."

Johnny ignored the comment.

Sharon, flushed from singing, didn't feel the cold until she stepped into the kitchen and saw the open back door. Tasha and Three Toes were gone. Sharon hurried out into the back yard. Three Toes lay on the ground, bleeding from a gash on her head. The crunch of footsteps on the frozen snow echoed in the dark. The breath caught in her chest. She reached up onto the shelf beside the door, and behind the jar of relish, her fingers closed on the gun Benny had insisted she keep. Sticking her head out into the night air, she did not display the gun in her hand, holding it at her side.

Herb stepped out from the shadow of a tree, one hand clamped around Tasha's mouth, a gun pointed at her head.

"No," Sharon gasped.

"No, what, fish kicker?" Herb taunted her. "No, don't hurt your little bastard?"

"You're crazy," Sharon snapped.

"Could be, but I got the gun, so you better watch what you say to me."

Sharon heard laughter inside the bar and the jukebox playing a familiar tune.

"Get down here."

"Let her go," Sharon said. "I'll do anything you ask."

"Fat chance. You're both going with me. Now get over here or I'll do you both right now, right here. Now, move it!"

"She's got nothing to do with this. Leave her alone. Take me. Just me."

"It's up to you, fish kicker. Either you play along or I finish it here."

Sharon looked at her daughter. "I'm so sorry, honey. It'll be okay. I promise."

"Move it," Herb snapped.

Three Toes whimpered and attempted to lift her head off the bloody patch of snow. As Herb looked down at the dog, Sharon resisted the impulse to shoot him, worried that his gun would go off and hurt Tasha. Before he looked up, she quickly shoved the gun into the waist band of her jeans under her shirt.

"Let her go," Sharon said again.

"No way. Now get over here, and if you try anything funny, I'll plug a hole in your darling daughter's head."

Sharon followed Herb as he struggled to keep hold of Tasha, making his way to the pickup he had parked at the edge of the parking lot. He lifted Tasha into the front seat. "Get in," he shouted at Sharon, the gun still pointed at Tasha.

Sharon climbed into the front seat of the pickup. Herb started the engine and quickly drove out onto the main road.

Tasha cried. "I'm scared, Mommy."

"I know," Sharon attempted to comfort her.

"Shut up, you two, or I'll plug you both right now and dump your bodies on the road." With one hand holding the gun pointed at Tasha and the other hand on the steering wheel, Herb lost control of the truck. The vehicle skidded halfway into the ongoing lane. "I don't want to hear another word from either of you," he shouted and then eased the vehicle back into the right lane.

Tasha tried to choke back her tears, but she couldn't help herself and the little girl continued sobbing.

"Whiny little brat," Herb shouted with a crazed laugh.

"Why don't you let her go? You only have a bone to pick with me. She has nothing to do with this." Sharon leaned forward, trying to get a read whether Herb might be sane enough to stop what she feared he might have planned. The glare of the oncoming headlights illuminated his face. His glassy eyes filled with meanness, his lips snarling. "Please, I beg you. Let my daughter go."

"I said shut up. If you keep yammering, you won't have a daughter to worry about."

Sharon leaned back in the seat. Her body throbbed with anxiety. Her head felt as though it would explode from trying to figure a way out of this situation. The road was a blur, and the moonlight had turned the snow cobalt blue. She thought about grabbing onto Tasha's arm and jumping out of the truck. Wherever they'd land would be better than what she feared Herb had planned for them. Fear of killing Tasha in the fall kept Sharon from grabbing the door handle and leaping out into the unknown and she decided to wait and hope for a better opportunity to get out of the grips of this maniac.

The pickup truck whizzed past a small shopping center. Herb turned off the main drag and continued up a poorly kept county road that led to a secluded camp ground. Sharon had stayed there a few days after she'd quit working at Willie's weigh station. Not many people knew about the place. An area set aside for tents wasn't much bigger than a turn-around in the road with a picnic table and a path that led to a lake that never got deeper than waist high.

Herb pulled the truck into the camping area and turned off the engine but kept the lights on. He reached under the seat and dragged out a rope. "Put your hands out kid," he said to Tasha.

The little girl looked at her mother, her cheeks now so wet with tears her face glistened in the dark.

"Stick your hands out. Now, damn it!" Herb shouted, his breathing shallow, his nostrils quivering.

Tasha slowly lifted her hands in front of her. Herb grabbed them, and tucking the gun under his arm, he tied the child's wrists together in a tight knot.

"No," Tasha protested. "That hurts."

"Shut up," Herb snapped and tied the other end of the rope securely around the steering column.

Sharon watched for any opportunity to grab the gun or to pull her pistol out and shoot him, but Herb had such a crazed look on his face that she feared he'd pull the trigger before she could get her gun aimed at him.

"Get out," he shouted at Sharon.

She opened the door and scrambled out of the truck. Herb quickly jumped out onto the ground and rushed around to the other side of the truck. Thankful not to have that gun pointed at her daughter, Sharon stood shivering in the cold.

Herb kicked the door closed. He turned on a flashlight and flicked the light toward the woods. "Walk."

"Where?" Sharon asked.

"Just move!"

Sharon looked back at the truck. She could just make out the top of Tasha's head above the dashboard as her daughter looked out at them. "What are you going to do?"

"You think you're such a smooth bitch. I'm going to turn you into an ice pop," he said and then let out a loud horselaugh.

The path around the lake was overgrown with barren berry vines and low-slung pine branches heavy with ice and snow, making walking difficult. Herb continued to poke the gun in Sharon's back, not so much to get her to move more quickly but because he seemed to be having a good time torturing her.

"How does it feel to be hunted and caught?" Herb jeered.

Sharon said nothing.

"I said how does it feel to be hunted and caught?" Herb jabbed the gun into her ribs.

"How the hell do you think it feels?" Sharon retorted.

The path ended in a small clearing, and in the murky moonlight, the remains of a recently built a bonfire was evident on the edge of the woods.

"Because of you, the cops came after me and I spent a couple freezing nights out here," Herb accused her.

"Suppose that's what you get for trying to burn down trailers while folks are sleeping. Did you really think you could get away with it? Sheriff Allan has had his eye on you since the summer. Not everyone is as stupid as you are."

"Shut your mouth." Herb threw the beam of the flashlight onto her face. "You look cold. I'd give you my jacket, but I don't want it to smell all fishy."

"What are you going to do?" Her teeth chattered uncontrollably.

"I thought you'd take a walk out on the ice."

"You're crazy."

"Maybe I am, but you're going to do more than freeze your butt off in a little while." Herb slid the light from Sharon's face out onto the frozen pond. "See how shiny and slick that ice looks. I wonder how far you could walk until you hit a thin spot? I hear there's a couple of big old turtles that bed down under there for the winter and the ice is thin in places because of the heat of their bodies. Anyway, that's what a sourdough told me when I was a kid. Never forgot that story, and I always wondered if it was true." Herb stepped closer to Sharon. The gun barrel glistened for a moment as it caught the glare of the flashlight. "It's slippery out there. Now mind you don't fall," he said and shoved her toward the icy pond.

Sharon knew winter hadn't been around long enough to freeze the lake solid. She took several steps onto the ice and then stopped.

"Got cold feet, fish kicker?"

She turned her back to Herb, took another step, and heard a slight tinkling as the ice gave way ever so slightly under her weight. Sliding her feet along the ice, she continued to move out toward the middle of the lake. Easing her hand up under her shirt, she took ahold of the gun stuck in her waistband.

"This is like the Ice Follies." Herb flashed the light across the ice in a zigzag motion. "Maybe you could dance for me," He let out a roaring laugh that echoed across the edge of the lake and back again.

Icy water seeped into Sharon's shoes.

Herb flashed the light onto her feet. "You're in the spotlight now, fish kicker. Why don't you give me a song? Sing like a freezing bird, and then we can all be happy that you had one last grand performance. Your personal show on ice." Herb began to laugh so hard he could not hold the flashlight steady. The beam of light scattered in every direction.

Several bursts of a car horn cut short his laughter, and he pointed the beam of light in the direction of the pickup truck.

"Okay, fish kicker, what are you going to sing?" He turned the light back into the middle of the pond where Sharon had been standing.

But she was not there.

He slid the light across the pond ice. "Bitch! Where are you?"

A constant blare of the car horn ricocheted off the surrounding woods. A lone dog barked in the woods. A strong wind blew across the lake. The branches of trees groaned and scratched against each other. Herb continued to scan the ice with his flashlight, and he stepped closer to the edge of the lake.

Then his flashlight caught her on the far side of the lake as she slithered backward across the icy surface on her belly with Benny's gun pointed at him.

"You think you can get away from me?" Herb pulled the trigger. Gunshot cracked across the pond as though a cannon had gone off.

The dog continued to bark. The car horn sounded again, and Sharon quickly slid to shore and scrambled into the underbrush.

Herb fired his gun again. The wind blew a slight smell of gunpowder across the pond to where Sharon was hiding.

"I'll get you!" Herb shouted.

From behind a tree, Sharon watched him step out onto the ice, sliding one foot out in front of him and then the other, the flashlight zigzagging beams across the ice.

He fired another shot and continued to cautiously step across the icy surface. She remained behind the tree, watching, knowing that as long as he was on the ice, Tasha was safe.

A crack came from the frozen pond. Herb stopped. Sharon held her breath and watched Herb attempt to scramble back to the shoreline. Before he reached the safety of solid land, there was a loud groan and the ice gave way under his weight. The night filled with what sounded like the breaking of a hundred windowpanes and the frozen lake shattered and broke open. The sound of a gunshot rang out, and then Herb slid into the freezing water.

"Help! Get me out of here!" he shouted, waving the flashlight frantically across the broken ice chunks and into the black night.

The lone dog barked frantically, the car horn continued to sound, and the freezing wind bit against her cheeks.

Herb desperately tried to pull himself out of the frigid water. As he struggled the ice cracked and broke away from his grasp. "I'll get you for this, fish kicker," Herb threatened. Another gunshot exploded. Herb screamed in pain.

The lake creaked and groaned, and the wind rushed across the frigid surface. Then, the night became deathly quiet.

Chapter Sixteen

SOMEONE PUT A FISTFUL OF coins in the jukebox, and one song after another played for more than an hour. The tunes sounded distant and hollow as the music echoed off the walls. Benny sat on a bar stool, his shoulders stooped, his hands cradling a bottle of beer. Johnny and Phil sat in the booth Julie usually occupied. Sheriff Allan sat across from Sharon in one of the back booths. Tasha had fallen asleep on the ride back to The Nowhere, and she now lay across the seat next to her mother.

The frigid air had penetrated Sharon's body in a way the cold had never done before. Everything she touched felt hot. The sheriff had wrapped her and Tasha in thermal blankets when he first arrived on the scene, and though the sleeping child no longer shivered, Sharon's teeth continued to clack together.

"By the look of things, you and Tasha are two lucky ladies." The sheriff removed his hat, set it on the table, took out a stack of papers, and began to take notes. "There's no doubt that he intended to do you both harm. I can't say that I've ever met someone as crazy as Herb."

The sheriff asked her to go over the story several more times, and she ached with fatigue.

"I still don't understand why you didn't put a stop to this and tell me what you saw that night."

Sharon sighed. "What I saw would have meant nothing in the courts. Two men from that distance could have been anyone."

"Maybe."

"And what do you think they'd have done with the testimony of a homeless fish kicker?"

Sheriff Allan cleared his throat, looked down at his notes, and wrote something down. He looked up at Sharon and was about to say something when his cell phone rang. He flipped it open. "Yeah." He got up from his seat and walked to the other side of the room.

Benny perked up and took a swig of his beer. Johnny's gaze followed the sheriff. Sharon leaned her head back against the wall. Tasha did not stir. Three Toes lay near the wood stove breathing softly, her head wound dressed with a crude wrap of gauze.

The sheriff closed his cell phone and returned. "They pulled Herb out of the lake. The fool still had the gun in his hand, though he's not going to cause any more trouble."

Tasha moved slightly. Her foot kicked out, and she softly whimpered. Sharon patted the little girl's legs and shushed her. "It's all right. Don't worry, you're safe."

Phil got up from his seat and came to stand next to the sheriff. "Why don't you let me take Sharon and Tasha over to my place? It doesn't sound like you'll be needing to drag any more information from her tonight."

"You're right." The sheriff gathered and picked up the papers and put on his hat.

Sharon stood. Phil leaned over. The child didn't make a sound as he lifted her up into his arms. Benny looked at Sharon. She thought he was going to say something but he turned back to the bar and lifted his bottle of beer.

Johnny scooted out of his seat. "I'll lock up," he offered.

Sheriff Allen slipped into his coat. "I got to go over and tell Herb's folks what's happened to their son. Some parts of this job really suck."

Sharon matched Phil's footsteps as he quickly walked across the icy road. She had never been so cold, and she wondered if she'd ever warm up. Tasha's head rested on Phil's shoulder, and in the glow of the yard light in front of the gas station, the big red mark on the child's forehead was clearly visible. She had banged it against the horn on the steering wheel in an attempt to help her mother. One little hand slipped out of the blanket, and Sharon quickly reached over and held on to the little fingers to keep them warm.

"She's one brave girl," Sharon said.

"Like her mom," Phil responded.

"I'm not so brave," Sharon disagreed.

"The hell you're not. And I don't know of anyone who could've out-smarted someone as crazy as Herb."

"Maybe, but a lot of good that's going to do me when Social Services takes Tasha away from me again."

"You don't know how this thing is going to turn out." There was such sincerity in his voice Sharon could have almost believed him.

Chapter Seventeen

CHRISTMAS WAS LESS THAN A week away, and so far, the snow-fall had been ordinary for Alaska. It snowed every day, and the roads were constantly being plowed and sanded. Huge drifts of snow covered small buildings. The shoulders of the roads were piled high, and mountains of ice and snow took up large portions of shopping mall parking lots where bulldozers had cleared areas for the holiday shoppers. The walkways were slick with ice, but everyone in Alaska knew how to maneuver across the stuff. Hardly any locals fell, and if they did, no one got hurt badly.

Sharon had the day off, and she drove into Kenai to do some last-minute Christmas shopping. She could have gone to Soldotna where there would have been more choices, but she felt a need to see the area again. It hadn't been but a month since she'd settled into a small house not far from her mother's place in Cooper Landing. She'd gotten a job as a carpenter's helper at the local sportsman's club in the middle of a major interior renovation, and she had enough money now to get nice gifts for everyone. And she could afford her own car.

Recently, her life had undergone so many changes. She wondered if her old haunts in Kenai had changed as well. Everything looked pretty much the same. The fabric store, the gun shop, and the VFW Hall were just as she had last seen them earlier in the summer. With only several days until the big holiday, tons of cars were parked outside those places. She hadn't intended on heading out north, but without thinking, Sharon kept to the road. She decided it would be nice to say hello to Phil and Beverly and drop by to see how Johnny was doing.

There wasn't much traffic, and a heavy wind blew thick drifts of snow across the road. There were no longer clear signs of where the road was divided, and Sharon had to keep her wits about her as she traveled. A large tanker truck raced toward her, and she knew the guys who drove those rigs got their jollies from seeing how fast they could go when the roads became thick with ice.

She passed the turn off to Willie's weigh station and wondered how he was doing. The poor old guy had quite a burden to carry these days, but Sharon wouldn't be surprised if he opened up for business as soon as the salmon were running again next summer. His wife would probably never be the same, and Willie would most likely not mention his son again. People around here liked him and trusted him. His weigh station would not lose any customers, and no one would dare to mention Herb in his presence.

Driving through the area brought back strong memories, and even with the huge mounds of snow along the shoulder of the road, Sharon recognized where she had spent most of her nights during the summer months. Funny how things turn out.

She continued up the road. Another tanker truck sped toward her. The trucker blew his horn and left a swirling storm of snow in his wake.

Phil had the gas station decked out in colored lights, and he'd plowed the pavement near the gas pumps down to the asphalt. Sharon drove into the small parking lot set aside for the mini market. Off to the left in the woods, she could see the remnants of the burned trailer. The snow had a dirty look where the wind whipped through the broken windows and blew soot across the ice.

Sharon got out of the car and opened the door to the mini mart. Phil sat on a stool behind the counter as he read a magazine. He looked up. "Well, look what the wind blew in." Grinning broadly, he put the magazine down on the counter.

"I thought I'd come by and wish you a Merry Christmas." Sharon removed her hat and gloves and felt the warmth of the wood stove on her skin. "Feels like old times."

"We miss you around here," he said.

"I miss all of you, too."

"Want some coffee?"

"Could use a cup. How's everyone?

Phil came from around the counter and poured two cups to the brim. "Same as usual."

"Has Johnny had any more of his stomach trouble?"

"No. And it's kind of funny, Julie took off for parts unknown a couple weeks ago, and since then, he's been just fine. It's almost as though that woman was his curse."

"When did she go?"

"Don't know. She never said anything to me. Johnny's got another woman who hangs around, but I think he's going to keep all females at a distance for a while. He's talking about selling the place, but I doubt he'll ever do that."

"And Benny, how's he doing?" There were several pickup trucks in the parking lot across the street, and Sharon suspected Benny's was among them.

"He's Benny. He comes and goes. He still blames himself for what happened to you. The guy can't get it into his head that you can't figure out what a crazy guy like Herb will do next. For a while, all he could talk about was how he should have done more to protect you. He's hit the bottle pretty bad again. He got stopped a couple of times for driving wild, but I think the sheriff took pity on him and let him go with a warning. I think that Benny's going to be hoofing it if it happens again, though."

Sharon finished her coffee. Coffee grounds lay across the bottom of the cup. "Nobody could have done any more than he did."

The late afternoon light had fallen away, and it was now a familiar winter dark. A calm aura glowed through the windows of the mini mart as the holiday lights blinked on and off.

"Suppose I'd better head back," she said. "I still have some shopping to do."

"I'm sure that Johnny would love to see you," Phil said.

Sharon headed for the door. "Give my love to Beverly and Linda. Thank you for everything."

"My pleasure." He reached over and grabbed several candy bars and a handful of small colorful foil wrapped Santa Clauses. "Here, slip these in Tasha's Christmas sock."

Sharon smiled, accepted the candy, and then stepped out into cold. A rusted pickup truck pulled in next to the gas pump. An old guy with a full white beard sat in the driver's seat, a regular at the bar. He gave Sharon a quick wave, stepped out of his vehicle, and went into the mini mart.

Sharon slid in behind the steering wheel and debated whether or not to go into the bar. She wouldn't mind seeing some of those folks again, Johnny in particular, but she was overwhelmed to think about all that had happened in the short time that she had worked there. Turning the key in the ignition and easing out of the parking spot, she still had not made up her mind. Backing up and then pulling forward, she spotted Benny's pickup parked on the far side of the lot.

"What are you afraid of," she mumbled and then drove across the street and parked next to Benny's truck.

She cleared her throat, took a deep breath, and climbed out of the car. A thick sheet of ice had formed over the gravel in the parking lot. A light dusting of snow began to fall, and a dim light glowed through the dirty windows. When she opened the door, she heard an old country classic was playing on the jukebox.

Nothing had changed. Benny sat on a barstool with his back to the door. Johnny leaned against the counter, talking to a young woman that Sharon had never seen at the bar before. Several grizzly regulars were playing poker in the back of the room, and two of Julie's girlfriends were sitting in their regular booth, watching the drips of condensation slowly crawl down their bottles of beer. There was a light on in the kitchen, but she didn't see anyone cooking.

Johnny saw her first. He gave her a big smile. "Well, well, come on in."

Benny glanced over his shoulder and then turned away again.

She hadn't seen Benny since she'd told him about moving back to the Cooper Landing area. He'd offered his place to her, and when she'd refused, he never showed up at the bar again before she left.

She walked across the dance floor.

"How's it going?" Johnny asked.

"Things are fine. I'm working, and Tasha's staying with me."

"That's great," Johnny said, and he glanced at Benny.

One of the women slid out of the booth and stood close to Sharon. "How's that little girl of yours?" the woman asked with beery breath.

Sharon stepped back slightly. "She's just fine."

"I'll bet she's pretty excited with Christmas coming in a couple of days." Listing slightly to her left, the woman took a hold of the bar. "Johnny, why don't you bring a couple more beers over to our table?"

"What are you doing this far away from home?" Benny asked angrily.

"Come by to wish you all a Happy Holiday," she said.

"Merry Christmas to you, too." Benny lifted his bottle of beer in a sarcastic salute.

"Can I get you something?" Johnny asked.

"No thanks," Sharon said and then she heard the familiar thump-thud foot steps of Three Toes. "How you doing, old girl?" She grabbed the dog's ears and rubbed them. "Tasha sure misses you."

"You'd have thought someone died the way that dog moped around after you left," Johnny said.

Sharon gave the dog a hearty pat on the top of its head. "I missed her, too."

"We all missed you," one of the poker players called out. She smiled.

"You missed my greasy cooking?"

"You bet."

Benny got up from his bar stool, reached over the counter, and grabbed up another beer. After twisting the cap off the bottle, he took a long swallow and didn't look at Sharon. The poker game started up again, and two of the players reached into their pockets for more money. Julie's old friends continued to sit in their booth, watching their beer bottles.

"Could I talk you into coming back and working in the kitchen?" Johnny asked.

"No," Sharon said. "Thanks, but no. In the spring, I'm moving to Anchorage and going to cooking school."

"Well, how about that. Benny, did you hear that? Sharon's going to be a chef."

Benny did not look at Sharon and took another drink from his beer.

"That's just great," Johnny said. "You have to come back and cook something special for us."

"Yeah, I'll do that." Looking around the room, she realized everyone had gone back into their own world. Even Benny looked lost in himself as he scooted his beer bottle from one hand to the other. "Think it's time I leave."

"I have a favor to ask you," Johnny said.

"What?"

"I'm selling this place."

Benny banged his beer bottle on the counter and then stomped out the back door.

"Some folks are not too happy about the new owners," Johnny said. "You know how it is. Change is hard around here."

"This is sudden," Sharon said.

"Not really. I've been thinking about it for some time." Johnny wiped the counter where Benny had been sitting.

"So, what kind of favor do you need from me?"

"I'm going to be on the road traveling for a while. I need someone reliable to take Three Toes. She wouldn't do well on the road. Some folks have taken an interest in caring for her. Even Phil said he'd hold on to her until I got back. But, now that I see her with you, I know where she belongs."

Sharon reached down and stroked the dog's head. "I think that would be just perfect. Tasha hasn't stopped asking for a dog since she moved in with me. She'll be thrilled."

"Good. Then it's settled."

One of the poker players slapped his cards down on the table and let out a belly laugh while the other player groaned. "That's it. I'm cleaned out." He stood, stretched, sidled up to the bar, and sat down on one of the stools. "I got enough for one more beer. Then I have to head home and face the old lady with my empty pockets."

Johnny opened a beer bottle and slid it across the counter.

"When can I take her?" Sharon asked.

"You can have her now."

"This would be one of the best Christmas gifts I could ever bring Tasha." She knelt down and scratched Three Toes under the chin. "You want to come home with me, girl?" Then she looked up at Johnny. "You sure you want to do this?"

"I'm sure. There's no doubt that you'll take good care of her. She needs more than just sitting around the wood stove all day. Being around kids will make her young again."

"How can I thank you?"

"Just take care of Three Toes. I know you will," Johnny said.

The other poker players were now lining up at the bar. "We need brews down here," one of them called out.

"Be with you in a minute," Johnny said. "You take care of yourself Sharon and good luck with that cooking school."

"So long, Johnny."

They shook hands. As she headed for the front door, Three Toes followed close behind. Sharon looked back at the bar. One of the women waved and blew Sharon a sloppy kiss. "See you," she called out.

A freezing wind lashed Sharon's face when she opened the door. The faint afternoon light in the sky had turned to purple, and a slight glimmer of the northern lights undulated overhead. The new fallen snow crunched underfoot. When Sharon opened the car door, Three Toes jumped in before her.

After Sharon got into the car, Benny came around the corner of the building and walked toward her. She rolled down her window.

He leaned in close. "It's not the same since you left." His beer breath made her nauseous.

She turned the key in the ignition.

"Maybe I can come see you some time," Benny said.

"Yes, maybe you can come see me." Sharon turned on the headlights. "You'll probably have lots to do when the new owners take over the bar."

Benny stepped back. "You take good care of that dog."

"I will," Sharon promised.

A tanker truck rushed past, leaving in its wake a huge cloud of snow and freezing slush.

Sharon started to roll up the window but then hesitated. "I'm sorry, Benny." His expression did not change. He turned and went back into the bar.

The drive back to Kenai felt long, and Sharon couldn't help but feel as though she had forgotten something at The Nowhere. Three Toes nudged her several times, but Sharon couldn't shake the loneliness that crept over her. She turned on the radio and sang along with the music, her mother's favorite, "Will The Circle Be Unbroken."

The headlights of the car bore a hole into the dark, and she found herself singing in a voice that she had not heard before. Lights in the oncoming lane rushed toward her, and for an instant, she frightened herself with the thought that this happiness she felt now would not last forever. She worried she'd screw up again. Then she had the upsetting thought that it might be best if she ended it all right then, there on the road back to Kenai. Then she'd never have to face another failure.

She thought about Tasha and Sharon sang louder and stronger. She sang until she was nearly screaming the words, and the more she sang, the more she wanted to live.

About the Author

MARGARET MENDEL lives in New York City and is a past board member of Mystery Writers of America and Sisters in Crime, NYC. She has an MFA in creative writing from Sarah Lawrence. Many of her short stories have appeared in literary journals and anthologies. For more than twenty years, she worked in the mental health field, though now she devotes herself to writing full time. She is an avid photographer and not only drags a laptop, but a Nikon D7000 camera wherever she goes. Read more about Margaret on her blog at: http://www.pushingtime.com/home/

Did you enjoy *Fish Kicker?*

If so, please help us spread the word about Margaret Mendel.

It's as easy as:

• Recommend the book to your family and friends
• Post a review
• Tweet and Facebook about it

Thank you.